SPRING Semester

A CAMPUS TALES STORY

Q.B. TYLER

Copyright © 2019 by Q.B. Tyler

All rights reserved.

ISBN: 9781070875262

No part of this publication may be reproduced, distributed, or transmitted in any form or by any means, including photocopying, recording, or other electronic or mechanical methods, without the prior written permission of the publisher, except in the case of brief quotations embodied in critical reviews and certain other noncommercial uses permitted by copyright law.

This is a work of fiction. Names, characters, businesses, places, events, and incidents are either the products of the author's imagination and used in a fictitious manner. Any resemblance to actual persons, living or dead, or actual events is purely coincidental.

Cover Design: NET Hook & Line Designs
Editing: Kristen Portillo—Your Editing Lounge
Interior Formatting: Stacey Blake—Champagne Book Design
Proofreading: Leslie Middleton

"...Two souls are sometimes created together and in love before they're born."
—F. Scott Fitzgerald

SPRING Semester

From the library of

elisalizzy

Prologue

Leighton

"WE REALLY SHOULDN'T KEEP DOING THIS, LEIGH." I watch as he pulls his jeans up over his pelvis, successfully blocking me from the glorious dick that was just inside me no more than four minutes ago. I stretch my naked body that's still sprawled out on my bed and rake my eyes over my best friend.

"But it's fun." I giggle and he glares at me. "Oh, come on, Everett, lighten up." I crawl across the bed to where he's sitting and rest my head on his muscular shoulder. "Why are you so tense lately? This about your chemistry class?"

"No." He grunts and stands up. "We are dating other people, Leighton. It's not fair to either one of them."

I fall back on the blankets and roll my eyes. "Hardly. You don't love her, and I'm literally only dating Adam because he does my statistics homework."

"That's not the point, Leigh." He runs a hand through his blonde hair, the curls wild and tousled in direct response from me pulling it while his mouth was between my thighs.

I hop off the bed and follow his hand through his hair, pushing it to the side like I love it and know he secretly does too. "Then what *is* the point? She won't even put out." I blink my ash colored eyes at him several times to drive my point home. *I put out. I've been putting out.* For what feels like one hundred years.

Okay four, but whatever.

Everett and I have been best friends since we were in fourth grade and he beat up a fifth grader for pulling my pigtails. He proceeded to walk me home every day for the rest of the year so no one would mess with me, and from then on, we were inseparable. And then six years later, our genitals became inseparable.

We're now in our junior year of college at Camden Graf in Washington D.C. after we both flew the coop of our small town in Arizona. My parents told me that I could only go this far if Everett came too, so we spent our entire senior year in high school studying—*and not just each other's anatomy*—and both of us received early acceptance.

But now at almost twenty, Everett and I are still doing the same shit, different day, and evidently, he's developed a guilty conscience.

Never mind that *he* got that blonde nightmare of a girlfriend first. What was I supposed to do? Sit around and watch them make out? I needed something…well, *someone* to pass the time until he got bored of her. *Just like in high school when he dated Arianna Drake.* The most popular girl in school, head cheerleader, Prom Queen—it was all so cliché I could scream.

But, to my surprise, Everett came to me after every date he had with her so I could erase her scent. This went on for all of three months before they broke up. He didn't date anyone our freshman or sophomore years of college, as we were basically glued at the hip, *literally,* with this newfound freedom of no curfew and being able to sleep in the same bed or be in each other's room with the door closed. Everett's roommate had an older girlfriend who lived off campus, so he was rarely there, which meant I basically became Everett's honorary roommate. And now, junior year, we both live off campus with our own bedrooms.

His blue eyes dart to mine, and I know by the size of his pupils that he's getting irritated with me. "I'm sorry I even fucking told you that," he growls and I purse my lips at his hostile comment. Lips that I know are swollen and red from his constant biting.

Everett Cartwright is the golden boy. The all-American lacrosse star, Prom King and social butterfly—*can we call guys butterflies? Whatever, he's perfect*. He does charity work… *somewhere*…and always tries to do the right thing. Everett, who is not only cheating on his equally perfect girlfriend, but doing so with his *not so* perfect best friend who he likes to bite and choke and fuck within an inch of her life.

"Because you tell me everything." I grab his ass as I walk across my room to pull on one of his lacrosse t-shirts.

"Is that mine?" He pulls his sweatshirt on over his torso giving me a tiny glimpse of his delicious V cut when his t-shirt rides up.

I look down and then up at him. "Yeah?"

"Why do you have it?"

"I don't know. I liked it." I shrug.

"Don't wear that around Alli." He grunts and I roll my eyes. "She already thinks we're fucking."

"Well, we are."

"*Were*."

"Sure, Cartwright." I pull my long, dark brown hair into a high ponytail. Hair that is now a complete rat's nest due to Everett's incessant pulling. Hair that Everett has told me on numerous occasions how much he loves. I'd caught him on many occasions submerging his face in my locks and breathing in my scent like it was his oxygen mask. I'd thought about cutting it, but Everett had gotten on his knees and begged—*both with his words and an orgasm*—to keep it long. So, now my hair is a few inches shy of my waist.

"I'm serious, we shouldn't keep doing this. It's not fair to Alli or… *Adam.*" He spits out his name like it tastes horrible.

"Why do you say his name like that?" I tuck a stray hair behind my ear as I power up my laptop to start my philosophy paper.

I meet his gaze just as anger flashes across them. "He's all wrong for you, Leigh."

"I know that. Did you hear the part about my statistics homework? It's not like I have you to cheat off of anymore. You had to go and take stats last year," I whine.

"I told you to take it with me. But we're getting off topic."

"What's the topic?"

"Are you sleeping with him?" he blurts out and the words hang in the air between us.

Do I tell him the truth? Or lie and keep him on his toes. Think quick, Mills. "What?"

"You heard me, Leighton Alexandra Mills. Are you sleeping with that tool?"

"Ooooh full name, are you going to spank me now?" I flutter my eyelashes at him.

"Answer me," he grits out.

"Would it matter if I was?"

If I didn't know any better, I'd say he looks hurt. Or maybe he's jealous. I know because I know what jealousy looks like. It spikes in my heart every time he goes skipping off to hang out with Alli after he's been with me. It's the look in Alli's eyes every time she looks at me when she realizes that he'd *just* spent the whole afternoon with me. Alli and I hate each other for the very same and yet different reasons. It's something I've pushed deep down in my soul and never let myself dwell on.

She doesn't love Everett, and I *do*.

He'll never want you like that. I hear *her* words as clear as day resonating throughout me.

"This is done, Leighton. We're done."

One

Everett

I STOP FOR A SECOND AFTER SLAMMING LEIGHTON'S FRONT door behind me. I'm half expecting her to run after me and tell me that she hasn't slept with Adam. That she's never let anyone touch her besides me. That she belongs to me. But then I remember my stubborn, sassy, sexier than sin best friend doesn't run after anyone. It's why men go crazy for her.

It's why I'm crazy for her.

I jog down her steps towards my Jeep before casting one last glance towards her front door. I'd barely thrown up a hand towards her roommate who was sitting on their couch with quite literally a cup of tea, ready to hear the latest in the Leighton and Everett saga. Skyler Mitchell is more perceptive than most and caught on to our dirty little secret within seconds of meeting us, which led to me bribing her with a years' worth of Starbucks to keep her thoughts to herself. She's the president of the "Leighton and Everett love each other" committee and made a point to call us out on it every time I try to sneak out of Leighton's bedroom.

Or when we have our sleepovers.

But she spent the first semester here banging her

professor, so she isn't really in any place to judge anyone for inappropriate relationships.

You're not in a relationship with Leigh, douchebag, my mind screams at me, and my dick immediately protests. *Why the fuck aren't we?*

My phone beeps breaking me from my thoughts and my heart sinks when I realize it's Alli, who also serves as a reminder as to why I'm not in a relationship with Leigh.

Alli Chem Lab: hiiii! what are you doing? *kissy face*

I toss my phone to the side, fully planning to ignore her for now, when my phone begins to ring. Feelings of dread flood me instantly as I press the Bluetooth in my car. "Hey, Alli."

"Babe, can you come with me to this mixer tonight?"

I let out a quiet groan as her voice comes through the speaker. "Tonight? I kind of have to study."

"It's Friday night, come on…" she whines. "By the way, where are you? I texted you a few times."

Translation: Are you with Leighton again?

"In the car."

"Oh…" I hear the question in just that one word. "Well, where *were* you?"

I let out a sigh. "Library." The lie comes out before I can catch it, and I wince at the fact that I'm being dishonest with her. But I'm tired of the same old *why do you hang out with Leighton so much? You see her more than you see me.* It's starting to grate on my nerves.

Then break up with her!

I know I did this to myself. I asked Alli out to trigger Leighton's jealousy but all it did was make her get a boyfriend of her own.

Fucking tool. I hate that guy. I grip the steering wheel thinking about him fucking her. About him kissing her. Touching her. Just…being near her.

All of it makes me irate.

She wouldn't sleep with him.

Tell me you're not sleeping with him, Leigh.

"Everett?" Her voice washes over me and I rub my forehead as I come to a stoplight.

"Yeah. I mean yes, I'll meet you wherever."

"A bunch of us are pregaming at my place. Come over early?"

"Yeah…okay. Sure." I pull into my parking spot outside of the townhouse I share with two other guys from the lacrosse team.

"Okay…and babe?"

"Uh huh?"

"Don't bring Leighton."

I walk through the door of my house to the sounds of cheering, and I turn the corner to see my roommates Pat and Dave playing Xbox.

"Hey, douchebags." I drop to the couch adjacent to them and prop my foot on the coffee table. A bong sits on top of it, taunting me, and if I was sure I wouldn't have a drug test this month, I'd indulge. I reach for the bag of Doritos next to it instead.

"How's the wife?" Pat asks without turning around.

"How's the cute Italian?" Dave asks and I groan thinking about Dave's obsession with Skyler.

"Skyler is still taken. And…Leighton is not my wife."

"Much to your disappointment," Pat interjects. "Which I don't know why you're so upset. You're sleeping with two chicks and the hotter one doesn't even care." He waves his arm as I watch Dave's team tackle Pat's. "OH, WHAT THE FUCK!"

I grit my teeth, trying not to let it bother me that he called Leighton hot. "I'm not sleeping with Alli."

They both drop their controllers and turn around. "Pause the shit," Pat says to Dave. "What?" Pat grabs the bong, lights it and takes a long pull. "You're not fucking Malibu Barbie?"

I roll my eyes and stand up. "I'm out of here."

"No, wait wait wait, don't listen to this asshole," Dave says. He looks up at me and then at Pat. "But…why?"

I shrug, as I think about why I've kept Alli at arm's length. *You know why.*

"Can you just man up and tell Leighton you love her, you pussy?" Pat turns back around. "Unpause, I've had about enough of him." They turn back to the television and I put both middle fingers up for each of them.

I climb the stairs toward my bedroom and flop on my bed before pulling out my phone.

Maybe I should call Leighton.

No fucking way, you always give in first.

"Fuck it," I grit out as I press her contact. She answers on the first ring and I can't stop the smile pulling at my lips that maybe she was waiting for me to call.

"Everett."

"Leighton."

The line is silent, and I swear I can hear her nerves through the phone.

"What did you mean when you said we were done? You mean you're done…with me?"

I hear the sadness in her voice and my traitorous dick immediately hardens as I picture her bottom lip jutting out as she twists a hair around her finger. "No. I shouldn't have said that. Of course, I'm not done with you. We'll always be friends, Leigh." I hear her sniffle and I sit up on my bed to listen closer. "Leigh, are you…crying?"

"No, you jerk, allergies."

I smirk. "You don't have allergies."

"Well…whatever. You were being an ass!"

The smirk falls and my eyebrows furrow in annoyance. "You wouldn't tell me if you were fucking some other guy!"

"Why does it matter?!"

"Because it fucking does, Leighton," I growl.

"No, okay! No, I'm not sleeping with Adam. But I guess I should since you're not going to fuck me anymore."

Backpedal, Cartwright. Backpedal! "I didn't…"

"You said we shouldn't do this anymore. So, what, you were just saying that to get a rise out of me?"

Yes, kind of. "Well, no—" I lie.

"So, you meant it?"

I rub a hand over my eyes. *This isn't going to end well.* "You're being a bitch, Leigh."

"And you're being a dick!" she argues back.

Nothing good is going to come from this. Get the fuck off the phone. "I have to go. I'll talk to you later."

"Fine." Click.

I let myself stew over my conversation with Leighton for an hour before getting up to shower hoping that it would help alleviate the tension of arguing with my best friend. I let my head fall back to allow the hot water of my shower to rain down on my face and my torso. My shoulders feel like they're in knots and my back feels tense and stiff. I hate fighting with Leighton; it makes me feel like I've physically gone to war.

My shower curtain slides across the metal, and my eyes immediately fly open in wonder of who the fuck is in the bathroom when Leighton steps into the tub with me.

My eyes widen even further when it registers that she's really here. *Looking like sex on a fucking stick.* "What are you doing?" I ask, though the ability to speak is slowly shutting down as I take in her perfect body. She is lean from soccer, and while it's her off season, she still trains three times a week with the team. My eyes scan over her face. Wide eyes that are usually lined with eyeliner and eyelashes that are always perfectly curled are now void of anything. A dusting of freckles covers her nose like she'd been sprinkled with cinnamon, and I watch as she scrunches it in that cute way she does when she's trying to get her way with me. I follow the trail to her cheekbones and her pout that is currently pursed, waiting for me to kiss her.

Her features are so striking, it takes me a minute to catch my breath around her. Her mother is from the Philippines and her father is from Scotland, giving her an exotic look that makes heads turn everywhere she goes. Her skin is naturally sun-kissed due to her Filipino roots which gives her a bronze glow at all times and it makes me want to run my nose all over her skin to smell the sun on her. I run my gaze down her body, wanting to touch her. Claim her. Defile her.

"I came to apologize," she whispers, "but from the way you're looking at me, it seems like I'm forgiven." I look up at her as her teeth graze her bottom lip. "I hate when you're mad at me."

"I hate it too." I move forward and lean down, pressing my lips to her collarbone and rain kisses across her chest to the other side. My hands grip her hips and I pull her flush against my chest, her hard nipples brushing against my abdomen and making my dick even harder.

"Kiss and make up?" she whispers and when I pull back, I see the devilish look in her eye. *Fuck and make up* is more like it.

"Fuck yes," I growl at her as I capture her mouth. I rub my tongue against hers, feeding her my apology the only way I can with Leighton. What we have is sacred, and I don't think it's a connection that will ever go away. I've never felt about anyone the way I feel about her. She's my best friend and at times I feel like the other half of me. She understands me on a level that no one else gets, and I hate the thought that one day someone could know her better than I do.

"You're in your head." She runs her hands up my chest and presses them to my heart. "And your heart is pounding. What's wrong?"

"Nothing, Leigh." I smile at her, not wanting to get into this now.

She pouts and wraps her arms around me, pushing her head to my chest. My cock rests against her stomach and it twitches when her smooth skin rubs against me. "I wouldn't… sleep with Adam or anyone…while we're…" She trails off. "I have more respect for you than that."

I don't say anything in response. Instead, I ask, "Are Pat and Dave still downstairs?" She nods as I note her trying to blink the tears out of her eyes. "Well, keep it down when you come, yeah?" I smirk at her.

"Oh, my fucking *GOD!*" she screams. *Yes, screams* as soon as my tongue moves across her clit. She screams like she's in a scene from *The Exorcist*. I feel her fingers moving against my scalp as she humps my face, trying her best to chase the orgasm I'm dangling in front of her like a proverbial carrot. "Jesus, Everett, *please*."

I dig my fingers into her thighs, the nails biting her flesh as I nibble at that space between her legs. She's always tasted like someone drizzled honey over her skin. Sweet, delectable, delicious. I went down on my girlfriend in high school, and she didn't taste half as good as Leighton.

Leighton also had an entire fucking fit when she found out, so overall that experience wasn't pleasant. She didn't talk to me for a week after, and I finally had to show up at her house when I knew her parents weren't home and pin her down to get her to talk to me. It ended with me eating her pussy for an hour and a half.

To this day, I still don't think she's over it.

"Come for me, baby." I slide my hands under her butt and grip her ass *hard*. I hear the *b* word even as it slips out, and I'm grateful Leighton is too close to her orgasm to hear it. I slide two fingers into her cunt as I continue to tongue her sweet clit. Her body goes completely lax and I smile as I witness her full submission. "Open your eyes," I command, and I watch as she struggles to pry them open, but finally does and they land on me and I see that her pupils are dilated and full of lust.

I know what I'm doing, and I know what I want to hear. I always want to hear it after we've fought, and I know the way to get it out of her. Her eyes well up with tears and I watch as one trickles down her face and I wish I could lick it away. I raise an eyebrow at her, as if I'm daring her to come and then she does. *Hard.*

"*Fuck. I love you,*" she whimpers as she grips the sheets underneath her.

And just like that, I can't wait another second to be inside of her. I've barely let her come down from her high when I'm inside her, my hand wrapped around her throat. "Fuck," I grunt. "You're still going. I'm going to lose it if your pussy doesn't cut that shit out, and I don't have a condom on."

"So?" she manages to gasp out and I instantly chastise myself for sliding in while she's still riding the high of an orgasm. She's likely to agree to anything at this moment. *Pull the fuck out, Cartwright.* I release some pressure on her throat and she sputters slightly as she tries to take a deep breath. "Come… inside…me," she manages to choke out and I pull my face out of her neck to stare down at her perfect face.

"Oh fuck…" I grumble as I feel the familiar tingle in my balls. "Leighton, I have to pull out."

"No!" she whimpers, and I screw my eyes shut as I feel it coming. "I want to come with you." I've constricted her breathing so her words are coming out breathy and slow and I know she's about to come again so I release my hand from around her throat. All it takes is two strokes across her clit when I feel her detonate. Her legs slide around me, her ankles locking behind my back to keep me in place as she falls apart in my arms. Her fingers drag down my back so hard I wouldn't be surprised if she pierced the skin. Her lips are on mine in an instant, biting and then kissing away the sting of her teeth. I come with a roar inside of her, my bed frame banging against the wall as I fuck her relentlessly.

When I manage to pull out, there's a trail of cum from my cock to her pussy and I watch transfixed as my cum leaks out of her. I resist the possessive urge running through my veins to push it back inside. I look down at her before I let my head fall to her chest. After a few moments, I ask her, "You haven't been irresponsible with your pill, have you?"

"No. Every day, three PM." And I feel somewhat better about our reckless sex. We typically use condoms, but every once in a while, we slip up and then proceed to spend the next week in a state of paranoia at the thought of an unplanned pregnancy. I fall back next to her in an exhausted heap, her legs tangling through mine as she snuggles into my side. "I meant what I said, you know."

"When?" I ask her.

"I do love you," she whispers, and I know the only reason she's saying it is because my room is slightly dark and completely quiet. The air is still and the only sound to be heard is our breathing. The moments just after we have sex Leighton is vulnerable, soft, and it makes me want to tell her everything. Her guard usually goes back up somewhere between five and ten minutes after, so I know I need to speak up if I want to keep her like this.

I love you, Leighton, let's give us a shot. I want to whisper these words into the quiet room as her fingertips trail up and down my arm.

"Leighton—" The sound of a cell phone interrupts me, serving as a harsh reminder that people exist outside of the two of us that may not be totally on board with us *giving it a shot.* I cringe when I realize it's *my* cellphone. I ignore it, knowing who it probably is when I feel Leighton moving away from me. "Wait."

"No, it's fine, I know you probably need to take it." I can't see her, but I can hear the pout in her voice.

I pull her body back to mine and tuck her into my side before I reach for the lamp next to me and turn it on. She squints at the sudden flash of light, and it illuminates the sex haze around us. Her cheeks are flushed, her hair is wild and uncontrolled, and there's a smile tugging at the corners of her swollen lips. Eventually the phone stops ringing, and I prepare myself to speak again when she speaks up first.

"Do you want to stay over tonight? Skyler is staying at Aidan's and Peyton went to party at Georgetown for the weekend."

My eyes jump to the clock on my nightstand and I know Alli is expecting me soon. *Fuck*. "I uhhh, I kind of have plans."

"Plans?" she asks, like any plans I have she should be privy to, when realization dawns on her. "I see."

"Hey." I reach for her chin and raise it up for me to look at her. "I'm going to break up with Alli."

Her eyes widen and she averts her gaze, letting them float around my room presumably because she knows I can read her the second our eyes meet. "You are?" For the first time, I hear it—the hope in her voice.

"Fuck." I grumble as I sit up and pull her naked body into my lap. My bare skin immediately takes notice and my cock jumps in response to her lush curves pressed right up against me. "You really haven't figured out what you mean to me by now?" She casts her gaze downward as she sinks her teeth into her lip. I grab her face, wanting to look at her while I finally tell her the truth. "Do I have to spell it out for you?" I whisper against her lips disallowing them to touch her but close enough that she can feel my breath. I push the strands that frame her face back and out of her eyes so I can search them for hesitation or doubt over what I'm about to tell her.

Her eyes flutter closed and her sweet voice surrounds me. "What...what about Alli?"

I rub my nose against hers. "You mean the girl I asked out to make you jealous?"

She flinches. "Seriously? Well…it worked."

I take a deep breath, preparing myself to speak the words aloud that I've kept to myself for so long. "It wasn't my smartest idea. Leighton…it's been *you* for so long."

"Me?" she squeaks and I know she's trying to stall.

"Yes. You." *Tell me you want me too, baby.*

I watch as the tears slide down her face and her eyes close slowly. When they open, they're so bright the water amplifies the honey flecks in her irises. "She said…she said you'd never…want me…"

"*Who* said that?" My brows furrow in question and irritation. Whoever said that clearly doesn't have eyes.

"Stacey Peters." She bites her bottom lip out of what I think is embarrassment.

"Stacey Peters? Like from high school?" *That stage five clinger that spent half of our senior year unashamedly sliding into my DMs?*

She nods. "She said you'd never think of me that way."

I snort. "And you bought that shit? You've dealt with bitchy girls. Hell, you speak fluent *bitchy girl*," I tease, and she narrows her eyes at me. "She was jealous, Leigh."

Her eyebrows shoot up to her hairline like it's the first time she's ever heard the theory that girls take shots at other girls because they're filled with envy. "Jealous?"

"Yeah, she wanted me, and I was so fucking into you. I *am* so fucking into you."

"You were?"

I chuckle and tap my fingers against her forehead. "God, you're dense."

"Shut the fuck up." She swats my hand away. "So, wait, why are you just saying something now?"

Because I was a chicken shit? I didn't think I was good enough for you? I didn't think you felt the same, and I didn't want to ruin our friendship? Take your pick, Leigh. "Well, you weren't exactly sending me signals that you felt the same."

"Before or after I spent half of my high school career on my knees in front of you? Jesus, Cartwright, how could you not see?"

"How could *you* not see?" I ask her.

She blinks her eyes a few times, like the fog has been lifted and she can see everything clearly for the first time. "I just never thought…I mean look at you…"

"I'm not following."

"You're hot."

"That does seem to be the consensus amongst the ladies." She raises an eyebrow at me, and I chuckle. "I'm kidding, Leigh, chill."

"But that's what I'm saying: guys like you date blonde, perky, pretty cheerleaders…the most popular girl blah blah blah."

"Who said that's what I want? Furthermore, where'd you get the idea that you *aren't* hot? Because I'm sure you've seen the way guys all but undress you with their eyes the second you walk in a room. I basically threatened to do bodily harm to Pat and Dave the first time they met you." They had been practically tripping over their dicks the day I moved in when she showed up in those tiny fucking soccer shorts with a bottle of tequila.

"Oh stop. They don't see me like that." She rolls her eyes and I snort at her naivety.

"Right, because I told them you were off limits. *Indefinitely.*"

She looks me over like she doesn't quite believe me, her gaze narrowed and skeptical. "Everett…"

"Leighton, I want to do this. I want to be with you. Do you want to be with me?" I look into her eyes, the color of onyx, as I see her lowering her guard. Her features aren't hard or rigid like when we're outside of this bubble. "Don't be afraid of… this. I'm not going to hurt you. I'm not going to break us."

Her eyes well up with tears like I've just spoken her greatest fears in two sentences. I wipe the wetness from beneath her eyes and pull her into my chest. "Say yes, Leigh. Please."

"Yes." She pulls away and stares at me. "Fuck yes."

Two

Everett

THE SOUNDS OF CARDI B SURROUND ME THE SECOND I WALK into Alli's townhouse. Her house has become notorious for her pregames—they are basically full-blown parties *before* the party, so I'm not shocked by the number of people here. My eyes scan her living room as I watch people trying to bounce quarters into a shot glass and two of my lacrosse teammates playing beer pong. I nod at them as I make my way into the kitchen where I assume I'll find Alli taking copious shots and selfies with her sorority sisters.

"EVERETT!" I hear my name squealed by a few different girls as I make it to the kitchen, and then Alli's in my arms, reaching up to give me a kiss. I quickly dodge her lips and manage to pull out of her grasp without completely embarrassing her. Her platinum blonde hair is curled and flowing down her back and her heavily made up blue eyes are bright and shining, probably due to too many shots. Her lips are bright red, serving as a reminder to keep them far away from any part of me.

"I'm so glad you're here." She giggles. "Do you want a drink?" She holds the red solo cup that smells of straight vodka up to my mouth and I take a step back.

SPRING *Semester*

"No…actually, Alli, do you think we could ta—go upstairs for a second?" I need to get Alli alone, and suggesting we 'talk' would be the quickest way for her to avoid me all night.

"Oh…" She smiles and raises an eyebrow. "Lead the way." I hear her friends all giggle and cheer, and as we leave, someone screams, "Wrap it up!" just as we make it to the stairs.

I roll my eyes as I follow her up to her bedroom and shut the door. I've only been in here a handful of times, and I'm certain this will be the last. I let my eyes roam over the room as I prepare myself to break up with Alli, and a twinge of guilt moves through me. Not for breaking up with her because fuck that. *I want Leighton.* But guilty for getting her involved in the first place. Alli is a nice girl, albeit a little clingy and annoying; she's sweet, and it's obvious she really likes me, and I'm about to break up with her after I've spent the last three months screwing the girl I'm in love with behind her back.

I feel like a fucking asshole.

But, I'm not an asshole. I care about people's feelings, and I hadn't intended to hurt Alli. I wasn't even planning to continue sleeping with Leigh once we started dating.

Alli and I had been dating two weeks when Leighton and I got drunk and accidentally reverted back to our old ways. And then did so three more times that morning.

She hops on the bed, bouncing a few times because the alcohol probably has her a little disoriented and cocks her finger towards me.

"Alli…" I trail off. "That's not why I wanted to come up here."

"Oh, come on. When are you going to fuck me already?" She reaches for the hem of her shirt when I hold up a hand. I've seen her tits when she flashed me—*and Dave and Pat, I might add*—but other than that, I've kept things to over the clothes action.

"Stop, Alli. You know what, I should go and we can talk about this when you're sober." I reach for the doorknob when I hear her shrill voice piercing the air.

"Wait! Talk about what?" She's off the bed and standing in front of me. Her arms are crossed and pushing her breasts upwards making her cleavage more defined. She bites down on her bottom lip, and despite the fact that it turns me harder than granite when Leighton does it, I feel nothing.

I pull at my ear, which Leighton says is my tell that something is bothering me. A sign I'm sure is lost on Alli. "This… us…Alli, it's not working."

"Wh—what? What do you mean?"

"This was fun but—"

"This was fun? What the fuck? *You're* breaking up with *me*?" I hear the inflection in her voice and I'm immediately irritated. Alli has a very high opinion of herself, which is great for her, but the Princess act is annoying as fuck.

I clear my throat in an attempt to mask the irritation. "Yeah, Alli, I am. It's not fair to either of us."

"What does that mean?" I don't say anything as I prepare to phrase this as delicately as I can when she snorts. "It's about *her,* isn't it?"

I close my eyes and pinch the bridge of my nose as I kick myself for letting this become about Leighton. "It's about a whole lot of things, Alli."

"Bullshit. This is about your co-dependent, toxic friendship with *Leighton*." She spits out her name like it disgusts her, and I bite my tongue to avoid saying anything.

"This is about doing what makes me happy, Alli, and about wanting to do the right thing."

She takes a step away from me and turns her back to me. Her shoulders are hunched up around her ears, and I can feel the tension radiating off of her in waves. "Do you love her?" she whispers. I don't say anything and when she spins around, I expect anger or rage but all I see is sadness and hurt.

"I never meant to hurt you, Alli. That's on me. I take responsibility for that, I just…I didn't know how to make sense of—"

"I get it." She puts her hand up and lowers herself to her bed. She looks up at me with tears in her eyes. "You do love her."

"Yes." My voice isn't low or nervous, it's strong and full of conviction. I may feel bad, but I'm serious about how I feel about Leighton, and I'm not going to downplay that to anyone.

"Why…why not me?" She doesn't look at me, her blue eyes fixed on the ground as she speaks her insecurities into the quiet room. "I care about you too."

You are the fucking worst, Cartwright. I let out a breath as I sit next to her on the bed. "I've never had a whole lot of control over my feelings for Leigh. You can't control who you love, Alli. I'm sorry I didn't realize it sooner." I know I'm skewing the narrative slightly, but I don't want to dig the knife deeper by telling her I had been *very* aware of my feelings for Leighton.

"Does she know how lucky she is? You've never looked at me the way you look at her. You think you're hiding it? You stare at her with stars in your eyes."

I want to tell her that I'm the lucky one, but I refrain from saying that or the fact that she should have never tolerated me staring at another woman. "I'm an asshole, and all I can say is I'm sorry, Alli, but there are a hundred guys that would die to be with you."

"Just not you…"

"You'll find someone, Alli…that looks at you like that." She doesn't say anything for a moment and I'm left wondering if this conversation is about to take an ugly turn. "Please don't hate me."

She lets out a breath and stands up. I can see the hurt written all over her face still, but I also see her guard sliding up. "Well, will you at least come out tonight? I don't want to tell all my friends I just got dumped."

"Al—" I want to tell her I don't care because all I want is to curl up in bed with Leighton and make love to her until the sun rises, but maybe I owe this to Alli.

"Please, Everett! You promised you'd go with me. I don't want to be the only loser without a date."

"You're not a loser, and I'm fairly certain a lot of your friends are single." *Not to mention a fraternity-sorority mixer is probably the perfect place to find a new guy.*

"Everett! I haven't asked you for much…and you're breaking up with me for another girl. I'm just asking that you give me tonight." Her eyes plead, almost begging.

"I'm not going to pretend we're together. No kissing, no touching, Alli. We're not together," I tell her. The last thing I need is to put up some ridiculous charade and having it get back to Leighton that we were all over each other at some party.

Fuck that.

"Fine, Everett." She doesn't say anything before she's through her bedroom door and out of sight.

This did seem to be a pretty amicable break up. I had expected Alli to throw things and pitch a fit and possibly hit me; it could have been a lot worse.

What's a few drinks at a frat house?

SPRING *Semester*

Holy fucking shit, everything hurts.

The throbbing behind my eyes is exacerbated by the fact that I'm seconds from puking. My stomach rolls the second I move my head, and I freeze as I wait for the nausea to pass. *Fuck, I'm hungover.* I try to move to my side, knowing that I always feel worse when I'm lying on my back and manage to knock into someone. "Fuck," I grumble. "Leighton." I want to cuddle up to her despite my hangover, and I frown when everything feels...*different.* Her hair feels different and her skin—bare skin that I know as well as I know my own feels foreign.

I open one eye and they almost fly out of my skull when I see who's in bed next to me.

Oh my God, oh my God, oh my God. I look around realizing I'm in Alli's bedroom and Alli is in bed right next to me, sleeping peacefully. I shut my eyes and pray it's a dream, but when I open them, I'm still in this hellish nightmare.

"WHAT THE FUCK?!" I yell as I sit up so quick it spurs my nausea. But the hangover doesn't have anything on the fact that I am currently naked in bed with a woman that is *not* Leighton Mills.

"Oh my God, owwww," Alli moans as her eyes flutter open. "Jesus, Everett, loud much?" She sits up and I realize that she is *also* naked when her sheet falls below her chest.

"What the fuck, Alli!" I'm off the bed and pulling on my boxers that I find on the floor next to the bed.

She puts her hands over her eyes and groans. "What do you mean, what the fuck?"

"Why are we in bed together? What the fuck am I doing here?" I wrack my brain as I try to remember what the hell happened last night that would have led me here, but I don't remember much after leaving Alli's pregame. "What happened?"

"We got fucked up." She chuckles. "We did a lot of shots."

"Bullshit. I think I had one beer at your pregame and one Jell-O shot."

"But you drank a ton at the frat." *Why the fuck would I do that?* I find my jeans and reach for my phone. I'm fucking irate when I can't find it. *When's the last time I talked to Leighton?*

"Where's my phone, Alli?" I snarl.

"I don't know! And you're really on one hundred right now. I'm going to need you to tone it down." She closes her eyes and rubs her temples.

"Focus! What happened when we got back here?"

"Well…I think that's obvious, no?" She looks under the sheet and then points at me and then back to her naked body.

Her implications blare in my mind and my heart begins to pound. "We did not have sex," I grit out. I don't know if I'm trying to ignore the writing on the wall or hold onto hope that things aren't what they seem, but the look on Alli's face proves that I'm only kidding myself.

"Yeah…Everett, we did."

Leighton's sweet smile flashes through my mind. Her writhing underneath me yesterday after we decided to finally take that step that both of us have wanted for far too long. Her whispering in my ear that she loved me just as she came around my cock. *I wouldn't fuck that up.* "No. I…I wouldn't have done that. There's no way."

"Really? A naked woman in bed with you, and you'd turn it down?"

"Unless you miraculously became Leighton, yeah. I would have," I growl, and her eyebrows shoot to her hairline.

"You were cheating on me with her, weren't you?"

"What the fuck was your first clue?" I snap. *I'm lashing out and I know it. I'm angry. Livid. Pissed. Not to mention violently hungover. I wanted to destroy everyone because I know the second Leighton learns the truth it will destroy us both.*

She lets her head fall and shakes it slowly and I start to regret blurting out my confession. "I'm so stupid."

"You're not stupid, Alli. You're just not *her*."

"Well, clearly last night your dick didn't care."

Bile rises in my throat and I swallow it down. *No. I wouldn't cheat on Leigh. Never.* I pull my shirt on and grab my jacket. "Fuck this. I don't believe you." I shake my head and run a hand through my hair.

"What?" She purses her lips.

I put a hand on my forehead to try and quiet the roaring headache that's getting worse by the second. "That we fucked? I don't buy it."

"I mean it's kind of obvious, Everett. I think you're in denial."

"I wouldn't...I *couldn't* do that to her." I hear the pleading in my voice, and I wonder who I'm trying to convince. Her or me.

Fire burns in her eyes and if looks could kill, I'd be a dead man. "But you could do it to me?" She scoffs and rolls her eyes. "You know what? This nice guy shit you put on is all an act. So maybe you should drop it now." She climbs off the bed without a stitch of clothing and pulls on a t-shirt. "Now, get out of my house."

Three

Leighton

THE SOUND OF MY BEDROOM DOOR CLOSING PULLS ME OUT OF my sleep. For a moment, I'm disoriented and I immediately reach for Everett, as I assume, he slipped into my bed after he was done playing nice with Alli.

Thank God, he's done with her.

I frown when I feel cool sheets under my fingertips, and I sit up slightly as the post slumber fog dissipates. I quickly remember what happened just before I closed my eyes and feelings of uneasiness ghost over my skin.

Everett's phone was off.

He'd stopped answering my texts halfway through the night and I never heard from him again. Now, it wasn't unheard of for his phone to die, but he knew my number as well as he knew his own, so he'd always found a way to contact me when that happened.

As soon as I sit up completely, my eyes find him sitting at my desk facing my bed but staring at the floor. His shoulders are slumped and his face is sad, defeated almost. Like the time our high school lacrosse team lost the state championship. He barely talked to anyone for weeks. *Even me.*

"Hey," I whisper. "What are you doing all the way over there?"

His eyes meet mine. They're vacant and lifeless and I watch as he closes them slowly and rests his elbows on his legs. He swallows before his gaze meets mine slowly. "I just got you… and…" He clears his throat. "Leigh, I fucked up…*I think.*"

Fearing the worst, I pull my blankets up around my chest as I try to protect myself from whatever he has to tell me. I'm suddenly freezing, goosebumps pop up everywhere, and I feel the tears prickling in my eyes. I feel like someone's standing on my chest and my heart might beat out of it with how hard and fast it's pounding.

He wouldn't. He said he wouldn't break us. He promised.

"Go on…"

"I don't know, Leigh. Something happened…" He rubs the back of his neck. "I don't really know what exactly."

"What the fuck does that mean?" I snap. The goosebumps have turned to full blown shivers, and now I feel my hands shaking beneath the blanket preparing for what he has to say.

"I…I woke up this morning and I…I was so fucked up last night, Leigh. Like drunker than the night of Brian's graduation party."

That night is a huge blur. I have flashes of him fucking me against Brian's father's two hundred-thousand-dollar Maserati and then puking my guts out into his mother's rose garden. Everett and I woke up the next morning on a completely deflated air mattress we must have popped in the night with hangovers that would go on to last two days. For him to say it was worse than that, means I may not even want to know what he has to tell me.

Yes, you do. Call it morbid curiosity.
Or maybe ignorance really is bliss?

Anxiety grips my throat and I feel like I can't speak. "Do…do I have to know?" I choke out.

"I'd rather you hear it from me than…anyone else." He looks down at his hands before looking up at me sadly.

"So, there's something to…" I swallow the tears that are forming in my throat. "…know." I let out a breath. "Just tell me you didn't sleep with her."

"I…"

I'll kill him. He hasn't fucked her this whole time, and NOW he decides to? After what happened between us yesterday? "Everett." My lip trembles and I shake my head. "You didn't."

"I…I don't know." He drops his head into his hands. "I woke up this morning and we were both naked, and I…" I don't bother to listen to the rest before I'm off the bed and rushing into the bathroom. I hear him moving behind me, but I slam my door in his face before he can follow me inside.

"GET OUT!" I scream through the door.

"Leigh…baby, please don't do this. Just talk to me." *Talk? Talk about fucking what?*

"No, GO!" I pound my fist against my door. "GO. I fucking mean it, Everett. I want you out of my house."

"I don't remember anything, Leigh!" I hear him say, and his voice sounds defeated, but I'm too angry to care. *Why would he do this? How could he do this?… To me?* "I can't say for sure, and Alli says we did, but I don't buy it. I was so fucking trashed last night. I don't remember anything!"

I fling the door open so hard I'm surprised I don't pull it off the hinges. "Is that supposed to make me feel better? Does that excuse everything? What? I'm just supposed to be so madly in love with you that I don't need to hold you accountable for acting like a drunk fucking asshole?" I shove him hard, though he barely moves an inch. "I HATE YOU!"

His face looks like I've just destroyed him with those three words.

Good. We're even now.

Hardly.

"Leigh, baby, just...listen to me, *please*. I love *you*. I've always loved you. You know I wouldn't do this...I would never hurt you."

"What do you call this?" I yell as I let out a breath. I shake my head, my body finally succumbing to the pain as the tears slide down my cheeks. "I used to see you as this person that would never hurt me. But this? This is bullshit. If you loved me you never would have allowed yourself to be in this situation. Why the hell were you even in bed with her? Why would you agree to go to her room? How...how could you do this to me? To us?" Her questions are coming in rapid fire, and I don't know what to say or how to explain that will make this easier. That will make all of this go away.

"I...I don't know, Leigh. But you know me..." He grabs my hand and puts it over his heart before I can wriggle out of his grasp. "You know I'd die before I hurt you."

"Well, I guess I'll start planning your funeral." I spit out before I snatch my hand away. I wipe the tears from my eyes and take a few steps away from him. "I should have known this would happen." I shake my head. "How you get him is how you lose him. I just never imagined I'd lose you on the night I got you."

His arms are gripping my biceps hard the second the words leave my lips. "You're not allowed to throw that shit in my face. You're not allowed to hold that over my head like I could ever be capable of doing to you what I did to Alli or *any* girl that I've TRIED to entertain while I deal with my feelings for you. That's not fair and you know it."

Fair? He's telling me what's not fair? "What's not fair is you telling me you love me and then hooking up with some other girl the same night!"

"I don't know that I hooked up with her, Leigh."

Does he think I'm stupid? "Bullshit. You two were both naked? Something happened."

He runs a hand through that silky, gorgeous head of blonde hair that I wish I was pulling on as he plowed into me. *No, Leighton.* "I can't…I can't say one way or the other. But I came to you. I could have lied. I could have tried to keep it from you."

"And if Alli wasn't such a vindictive *cunt* that is probably chomping at the bit as we speak to get to me, you probably *would* have kept it from me. You knew Alli would blow your cover. Don't try to pretend that you're telling me because you're trying to do the right thing, Everett." I snort.

"It is! When have I ever lied to you? About anything!" The words explode out of him.

"I don't know, you tell me?"

"Look," he growls, "I get you're pissed, and rightfully so, but don't be childish."

"I'M BEING CHILDISH?"

"Yes, Leighton, you are. You know damn well I've never lied to you. Ever." His voice is hard and cold and for a full minute, I swear neither of us blinks as we hold each other's gazes. Finally, I look away.

"Fine." I move towards my bedroom door and open it. "I still need you to leave."

"Wh—what?" He takes a step back and a part of me hopes that he doesn't try to fight me on staying. That he gives me the space I need. *Hell, that he probably needs too.*

"I need you to go." My voice wavers, lacking conviction,

and I know all it will take is one *"Leighton,"* for me to let him stay. *I'm not strong enough for this.*

As if he can hear my thoughts, I feel his hand on my cheek. "Leighton…"

Be strong. Don't let him suck you in. "No!" I cry, the tears sliding down my face and I push his hands away. "No…you…you have to go. I need time. I need space."

"From me? Leighton, she doesn't mean anything. I told you that." His voice is pleading and I know I need him to go before that tiny voice in the back of my mind that is begging me to believe him starts to get louder. I needed space away from him to clear my thoughts and I can't do that while his blue eyes are staring into my soul like he knows every inch of it.

"It doesn't matter, Everett. You told me you weren't going to break us. You promised! And you did on the first fucking night."

"Please, baby…just…can we get past this? Tell me what I can do, I'll do anything," he pleads.

"There's nothing you can do, Everett. And I don't know if we can." I shake my head as I avoid his gaze. "I'll call you."

"When?"

"When I figure it out. When… it doesn't hurt so much." I close my eyes and smell his cologne in my personal space. "Please…don't." I back up against the door, but I feel his presence surrounding me.

"Look at me, baby."

"No…please," I whimper and I hate the sound of my voice. I sound so pitiful and weak.

I hate it.
I hate him.
I hate myself.

"Please," he whispers and I can feel his breath on my lips. "I'm so sorry I did this." My eyes open and I feel the gaping hole in my heart constrict. "Tell me how to fix it." His hands cup my cheeks and I let myself melt into him. If I were stronger, I'd push him away. But I just want to pretend this isn't a problem. I want to pretend that this won't be lurking in the corners of my mind every time he doesn't answer my text or any time he's out without me. For a second, I just want to be Leighton and Everett, two people that have loved each other for so long and can finally be together.

I don't want to be strong; I just want him to love me.

It's unfair, really. For the world to dangle him in front of me like this only to rip him away in such a cruel manner. I hadn't known karma to come back around *that* quickly. That's what this is, right? Karma? I slept with Alli's man, so she slept with mine?

"I don't know that you can fix this, Everett." I look up into his eyes the color of the ocean and the pain reflected in them mirrors mine. "Please…just go."

His shoulders sag with defeat. "Call me…please, Leigh."

I don't say anything as I watch him head down the stairs slowly. I wait until I hear my front door close before I drop to the floor and a sob so loud and painful rips through me.

"Fuck him, seriously," Peyton White, my other roommate, says as she props her feet up on our coffee table. "And seriously fuck him for making me cut my Georgetown weekend short. Those Beta Pi guys sure know how to party." She takes a sip of the rosé straight from the bottle before passing it to me. I'd summoned both her and Skyler home with an SOS the second

I managed to pull myself off the floor, and in true best friend form, they both came running. Despite the fact that Skyler had a romantic weekend planned with Aidan, and Peyton probably had a similar weekend planned with an entire fraternity, they came when I called.

Skyler enters the room with a second bottle of wine, a pint of ice cream, and at least two blankets under her arm. "We don't know for sure that he slept with her and if he was *that* drunk then he more than likely had whiskey dick…" I shoot her a glare. "IF they even tried anything!"

"That is *so* not the point!" Peyton argues. She itches her nose ring and runs a hand through her blonde hair before pulling it up into a bun. "Why was he in bed with her?"

"Hello!" I point at Peyton. "Thank you?" I look at Skyler as if to say, 'argue that point, please.'

Skyler blows a light brown hair from her eyes and rubs her lips. "Maybe he was just so drunk, he needed a place to pass out?"

"Naked?" Peyton rolls her eyes. "That can't be your only argument."

Skyler opens the pint of ice cream and hands it to me with a spoon. "I'm not being naive! I'm just…" she looks around the room, as I assume she's trying to find the right words. "Everett is so crazy about you." She looks at me, and I stare down into the cup of mint chocolate chip. "He loves you so much. He always has! Have you seen the way he looks at you when he thinks no one is looking? Have you seen the way *you* look at him while *everyone* is looking? You two belong together."

"Maybe, but the right guy at the wrong time is still the wrong guy," Peyton argues.

My heart sinks hearing Peyton's words. *What does that mean? I have to wait even longer to be with him?*

Do I even want to be with him now?

"I agree that maybe you need some space to process this. But if you're still unsure in a few days, I think there's a reason for that. Be honest with him, Leighton. You guys might be dishonest with everyone else in your life," Skyler says with a pointed look, "but you've always been open with each other."

I nod as I take a bite of the minty dessert, and for a second, I pray it heals the pain in my chest. "Am I being silly? I mean, do I have the right to be mad if he slept with her?"

"Uh, yes?" Peyton interjects. "Sky said he almost took the door off the hinges when he was leaving yesterday because he thought you were sleeping with Alan!"

"Adam," I correct.

"Irrelevant! I literally met the guy twice. Couldn't even pick him out of a lineup," Peyton says as she picks at her nail beds.

"He's in our statistics class!"

Peyton grabs the ice cream from me and takes a bite. "So?"

"Oh my God, off topic. I've never slept with Adam." I tell them.

"And he said he never slept with Alli. You also said that he was just trying to make you jealous," Skyler says. "So, what reason would he have for sleeping with her *now*?"

"What reason do fuckboys have for doing anything? The reasoning is in their name! They're fuckboys!" Peyton retorts.

"Everett is not a fuckboy!" Skyler furrows her brow, and if I didn't know any better, I'd say she was related to him with the way she's defending him. "He's kind and caring and considerate and worships the ground Leigh walks on! Literally. I think if she asked him to, he'd kiss the ground beneath her feet."

Peyton takes another sip of wine, and her hazel eyes roll

in a full circle. "Look Leigh, you know whatever you choose to do, I've got your back one hundred and ten percent. This is a judgment free zone…I just…I don't want to see you getting hurt, and I know it's easy to get tunnel vision when you're in love."

"I know." I take a sip of the rosé and let the bubbles trickle down my throat. I know Skyler and Peyton are just trying to help, and I'm grateful that they are arguing both sides. If they were both for or against working things out with Everett, I don't know how I'd be able to remain objective. Skyler is Team Everett and Peyton is certainly not, but first and foremost I know they are both Team Leighton, which is all I could ask for in my best friends. Best friends I want to get drunk with and forget about this horrible day. *Like now.*

I take a long swig from the bottle, swallowing the rest of the alcohol. "Can we get something stronger than this?"

Four

Everett

A BILLOW OF SMOKE SURROUNDS ME UNDER THE LOW lighting of our living room. The sun is just starting to set, on what is quite possibly the worst day I've had in years, creating a yellowish glow on the walls through the window. Pat's been seated next to me for the past ten hours since I got back from Leighton's this morning trying to snap me out of the trance I'm in, but nothing has worked.

"You sure you don't want a hit?" He holds the bong in front of me and for a moment I consider taking a hit and sending my future as starting attacker and lacrosse captain next year up in flames alongside my future with Leighton.

I sigh. "No."

He reaches forward and grabs a slice of the pizza we ordered earlier that he all but shoved down my throat knowing that on top of everything I was battling a massive hangover. "You really don't remember?" he asks for what feels like the millionth time, and my head snaps to his.

"No, Pat, I don't," I growl.

"Shit. You must have been really trashed."

"I don't know what would have possessed me to get that fucking drunk, knowing Leigh was waiting for me to come back later." I lean my head against the back of the couch and let out a groan. "She's so fucking pissed at me."

"She'll come around, dude. She knows how you feel about her."

"That's what makes this so much fucking worse. If this were a week ago, she'd be annoyed, but she wouldn't hate me. She wouldn't be rethinking *us*. I'm going to lose her, man." The words make the dull throb in my chest flicker to life again. My heart begins to pound faster, and I feel a wave of nausea roll through me.

She has to forgive me.

"You're not going to lose her. You two are…" he takes another hit of the bong, "I don't know, man; I'm pretty high but…like the real deal or whatever." He takes a long swig of his beer. "You wanna go out?" His shaggy brown hair falls forward and he sends his hand through it to push it back.

"Do you think I'm in *any* mood to be around a bunch of fucking people?" I pull the hood of my CGU lacrosse sweatshirt up over my head and cross my arms, fully prepared to sulk for the rest of the evening when Pat puts his phone up in front of my face.

"You sure about that?" I stare at Skyler Mitchell's latest Instagram upload. It's a picture of Skyler, Leighton, and Peyton at one of our mutual friends, Seth's apartment. He'd mentioned having a pregame before possibly going to bars later, but I ruled that out the second I left Leighton this morning

She's going out?

In the picture, Leighton is downing a shot while Peyton appears to be cheering her on as Skyler cheeses for the camera. Their personalities in a nutshell. It seems like a candid photo but the fact that Skyler posted it, tagged Leigh, and where they are means they wanted *me* to see this. I know how to read subtweets, and even more importantly, I speak fluent Leighton Mills.

Leighton wants me to know where she is. She wants me to come for her.

"I'll be ready in thirty."

"Alright! Let's go get your girl! I'm going to text Peyton to make sure they stay there." Pat downs the glass of water sitting in front of him.

"That the only reason?" I raise an eyebrow at him.

"Okay, and maybe because I'm trying to shoot my shot." He glares at me. Pat has been trying to get with Peyton for quite some time, and despite the fact that Peyton's standards seem lower than low, she's managed to keep Pat out of her pants.

"For the millionth time."

"Hey, you want to suck my left nut? You're not in any position to be giving out advice on women right now, douche."

Dave, who isn't privy to the events of the night, comes walking through our door just as I grab a beer from our refrigerator. He's been at the library all day and I can tell he's ready to cut loose after staring at biology bullshit all day. I, on the other hand, don't want to be hammered when I see Leigh, not to mention the room has just stopped spinning about twenty minutes ago, so I'm not in any rush to get drunk again, but I know I need something to take the edge off.

"We going to Seth's?" Dave steps into the kitchen and grabs a piece of pizza from earlier and a beer from the fridge. "Give me ten minutes to get ready."

"Yeah, we're going so E can get his girl back," Pat tells him.

"Which girl?" he asks as he pops the can of a Natural Light beer.

"The only one he claims," Pat answers.

"What's up with Leigh?" He looks back and forth between me and Pat.

"Long story," I tell him.

"Cliff notes." Dave bites into his pizza as Pat looks at me.

"Leigh thinks he fucked Alli."

"Last night? Did you?" Dave narrows his gaze at me and I'm sure he's recalling our conversation from just yesterday where I told him I'd never had sex with her.

"He doesn't know," Pat answers and I shoot him a glare.

"What do you mean you don't know? Like you don't remember?" Dave pulls his glasses from his face that he uses while he's staring at a computer for long periods of time. He shakes his head. "Shit, I knew she'd be a boring lay."

"No, I just...I was fucked up, and I don't remember anything. I woke up this morning and we were naked in bed together."

"Fuck, dude. And you told Leigh?" He asks it in a way that reads more like *why the fuck did you tell Leigh?*

"If I didn't, Alli would have."

"And this is after you guys told each other you loved each other and all that shit?" Dave asks and I nod as he pieces everything together.

"You see why she's pissed?" I ask him.

"Shit, well, I saw Skyler's post, and I'm always down to see her, so I'm in." Dave downs the rest of his beer and crushes the empty can on the counter.

"Don't take all fucking day," I growl at him as I make my

way up the stairs to shower. Although, I'm somewhat grateful that they're coming with me; they'll distract Skyler and Peyton and maybe give me a chance to be alone with Leighton.

Here's hoping.

I briefly wonder if I'm making a huge mistake by showing up to this pregame when Leighton said she wanted space. *But then why would she go to our mutual friend's house? Knowing there was a chance I'd show up? And let Skyler post a photo?*

She wants me to come for her. She wants me to fight for her.

I nod at my reflection in the mirror before I pull off my clothes and step into the scalding hot water for the second time today.

I'm coming for you, baby.

By the time we get to Seth's house, it's almost eleven PM, and the party is no longer pregame status so I doubt we're going to bars because this has become a full-on house party. The second I walk in, Dave and Pat are on their respective missions, and I'm left searching for my girl. I'm grateful that I've always kept Alli from mingling with my friends too often, so I'm not worried about running into her. Alli is heavy into Greek life and, for the most part, my friends aren't.

I make my way through the crowded foyer and into the kitchen where there's a line for the keg, and my eyes immediately find bare skin that's practically glowing. It's barely April, and Leighton's entire back is out. The white silk top she's wearing reveals her smooth, toned back with two strings tied together in a neat bow behind her neck. Her long, thick hair is pulled into a top knot, exposing so much skin I want to gouge the eyes out of every guy here just so they can't feast their eyes on her. I rake my own eyes down her body to find tight black jeans tucked into ankle boots, and all I can picture is every piece of clothing she's wearing scattered all over my bedroom floor.

I watch as the guy fills her cup to the brim, his eyes unashamedly perving all over her, and I flex my fist. I watch as he whispers something in her ear and she giggles, and under normal circumstances I would breathe a sigh of relief by her fake as hell smile and her even faker giggle, but all I can see is red as his hand finds her back and runs his fingers down her skin.

I will literally break your shit off, dick.

I'm through the line before I can think and pulling her into my arms. "Everett?"

"I *know* you know better than that," I growl at Seth's roommate.

"E!" He smiles, like he hadn't just blatantly been feeling up Leighton. Like he hadn't been breaking the only bro code I adhere to. *Do not fuck with someone else's girl.* "Seth said you weren't coming!"

"So, you decided to make a pass at Leigh?"

"Everett, stop it. You're being a dick." She pulls out of my grasp and shoves at my chest before she storms away. I'm immediately following behind her into a corner, ignoring the douche at the keg, and I say a silent prayer as I plan to enter my own circle of hell.

"Peyton, Sky." I nod at them and Peyton glares at me before taking a long sip of her drink. Her red lips form a straight line and she scrunches her nose at me.

"Cartwright," she bites out and my eyes immediately float to Skyler, someone I'm praying will be my alliance in all of this.

Help. I try and tell her with my eyes.

She blinks her eyelashes several times and tucks a strand behind her ear. "Come on, Peyton let's go dance." I hear the implication. *I'm trying. But you gotta work for it.*

"And leave her with him?" Peyton points at me before she looks at Leighton. "Is that what you want?"

Leighton's eyes dart up to mine. "What are you doing here?"

"I...I wanted to see you. I love you," I blurt out, and I watch as Skyler's eyes almost bug out of her skull making me wish that all I had to do was win Skyler over. I've only met Aidan a few times when we'd all been at Leighton and Skyler's, but it seems like he's turned Skyler into a true romantic.

Thank God. I'd be dead if all she had was cynical ass Peyton.

Although, I watch as Peyton's eyes soften slightly before looking at Leighton. "I'm going to go take a shot. You want, Leigh?"

Leighton shakes her head. Before I can blink they've left us alone, and for the first time maybe ever things feel awkward between me and Leigh. I clear my throat before I lean in closer and whisper, "Do you want to go somewhere quieter?"

She visibly shivers and I watch as the goosebumps pop up all over. I smile to myself as I watch the effect I have on her. "Don't get cocky. Just because my body responds to you doesn't mean my mind and heart are on the same page." She takes a step back. "Don't touch me," she whispers.

I swallow and nod. I don't know how I'm going to respect her wishes, but I follow behind her as we make our way up the stairs and into Seth's bedroom. I peek my head in the connecting bathroom just to make sure no one is around before I let out a sigh of relief.

Alone, thank God.

"Talk." Her words slice through the quiet and the mounting tension between us and I turn to look at her. She's standing against the door, her arms crossed over her chest, a look of anger, pain, and worry across her face.

"I made a mistake," I whisper. "But it's over. Alli and I are over."

She snorts and rolls her eyes. "Great."

"Leigh…"

"What happened? How…how could you sleep with her?"

"I don't know…and I still don't remember any of it." I hate to keep using that as an excuse, but I have spent the majority of the day trying to jar my memory and I've come up empty every time. *Maybe we tried?* But based on how hard I blacked out, there was no way I could have stayed hard long enough to fuck her.

"That's not an excuse! What does that matter? What would you do if I slept with some other guy? What would you think if I told you I slept with Adam? Or woke up in bed naked with him? God, you flew off the handle when Rob touched me just now KNOWING that I wouldn't touch him with a ten-foot pole." She stamps her foot. "You'd be losing your mind if you knew I'd slept with someone else. And I'm supposed to accept that you fucked Alli *or whatever* because you tell me you love me and you ended it with her?" She scoffs and begins to pace the floor angrily. "That was certainly one hell of a parting gift."

"It wasn't like that, Leigh. I don't know what possessed me to go back to her place after we went out. I broke up with her before we even went out, and—"

She stops in her tracks and glares at me and immediately I know this isn't going to end well. "WHAT? Wait…" She puts her hand up. "You broke up with her and then still went out with her to some *sorostitute* shit? How desperate can she be? How dumb can *you* be?"

"I...I don't know. I'm sorry...I just thought I owed—"

"Owed? You didn't owe her shit. You guys spent three months making out and holding hands. Jesus Christ, Everett. Sometimes, I really resent this nice guy bullshit. Grow a pair, seriously."

I let out a breath, steeling myself for bitchy Leigh to make her presence.

Don't fight back. Just take it. She's just angry. And Leigh only knows how to fight one way. Dirty. As. Fuck.

My jaw ticks as I remember this fight isn't going to lead to makeup sex.

"You have something you want to say?" She stares at me, daring me to challenge her. Her black eyes narrow and her lips purse into a scowl.

"No," I tell her. "Leigh, I'm sorry. You have no idea how sorry I am for fucking things up between us." I sit on Seth's bed and stare up into her angry eyes. "But...are you ever going to be able to forgive me? You're...my best friend and...fuck, like the best person I know. You've been the most important person to me since we were what...fucking nine? If you're going to tell me this is it, then I need to know now so I can...I don't know...try to figure out what the new normalcy is," I gulp, "without you."

The words come out harsher than I intended. I know full well that Leigh probably needs time. Time I'll give her if she asks for it. I hadn't intended for it to sound like *it's now or never*. But she doesn't bite back. Her lip trembles and then it's between her teeth. "If I'm your best friend, and the best person you know how...how could you do this? You made me feel like I'm not enough." She fidgets with her hands and stares at the ground, one of the signs that she's embarrassed and I'm off the bed in an instant to try and combat her humiliation.

"Stop," I tell her.

I reach for her wrist and turn it over, running my finger over the tattoo she has there. The one that matches the one I have on my ribcage. Hers said *no matter where* and mine said *no matter what*. My parents went through a nasty divorce my senior year of high school and the night my dad moved out, Leighton showed up at my house with a fifth of Bacardi and the idea to get matching tattoos.

We shook on it…*well, fucked on it,* and the next morning we had permanent ink solidifying our friendship forever.

I bring her wrist to my mouth and run my lips over the skin. "No matter where, no matter what," I murmur and she gasps at the intimate touch.

"I…I told you not to touch me," she whispers, but I hear the conviction leaving her voice. She sounds fragile, scared, and not like my strong, brave girl. I hate myself for doing this to her. To her self-confidence. "I knew I'd crumble if you touched me." Her eyes are glassy and I wonder if it's out of sadness or because of the shots I'm assuming she had before I got here.

"Because you know how I feel about you." I lean down and press my forehead to hers. "Please…please forgive me. I want this…I want us."

Her lip trembles and I go for it, hoping she won't stop me. I cup her face and slowly swipe my lips across hers. She sighs against my mouth like she's been carrying the weight of the day around and she's finally letting it go. "You can't…you can't do this to me again."

"Never. Fuck. Never." I push her hard against the door and wedge my thigh between her legs knowing she loved to rub against me. "Can I take you home?" I ask her as I tug on her bun offering her neck up to me. I press my tongue to her pulse point and draw lazy circles with the tip.

She swallows and I feel her nod against my lips. *Fuck. She's forgiving me.* I pull back to look at her and give her the biggest smile.

"You're not off the hook, Cartwright." She furrows her brows. "And you're buying me pizza."

We make it back to her townhouse and despite the fact that she's drunk and spent the entire ride home practically in my lap, I kept my hands mostly to myself. We picked up pizza on the way home, and we are barely through the front door before she's biting into it. "Did you eat before you went out?"

She winces and shakes her head as she kicks off her shoes. "No."

"You know I hate that shit." I shoot her a glare and she shrugs sheepishly as she sits on her couch and puts her feet on her coffee table. I sit next to her and drape her legs over my lap to bring her closer to me. I pull her hair from the bun and the few bobby pins, letting her hair spill out over her shoulders. I press my lips to her bare skin and she leans into my touch.

"I…I think we should take it slow." Her lips speak but her body is saying something different entirely. Her legs are pressed together and her cheeks are growing pink under my gaze.

"You're saying this to the guy that literally rimmed you till you cried."

She scoffs and pushes me back. "I did not cry."

I chuckle. "I'm kidding, well not about the crying thing because you did. But we can take it as slow as you want, baby. Whatever you want," I whisper. "I'm just…happy that you don't hate me."

"I could never hate you," she tells me.

"You said it earlier…" I recall her words that have been ringing in my head since she spoke them.

"I didn't mean that."

I nod. "I wouldn't be surprised if you did. I almost ruined everything."

She shakes her head and pulls her hair over to one side like she does when she's nervous. "Let's not talk about it."

I know Leighton well enough to know this isn't over, but I also know she's drunk and my time with her before she's ready to pass out is numbered.

"Just promise me something?"

"Mmmhm?" She leans her head on my shoulder and I press my lips to her forehead.

"Don't push me away in the morning."

The feeling of someone moving pulls me out of my sleep, and I see Leighton pulling her hair up into a ponytail. I'd carried her up the stairs to bed last night and managed to get her undressed and in some sweatpants and a t-shirt—*both of which belong to me*—before I succumbed to sleep beside her. I had contemplated waking her up to fuck her senseless, but I wanted her to be sober and more importantly sentient before we opened that door again.

"Hey." I stretch my hands up towards the head of her bed and sit up slightly. "It's early, come back to bed."

She narrows her gaze at me. "I think you should leave."

"What?"

She shakes her head and leans against her desk. "This didn't make everything better, Everett. You preying on me while I'm drunk and vulnerable doesn't mean everything's okay. I was pretty wasted by the time you saw me, and I let your sweet words and touches convince me that I was over it. I'm not, Everett."

I sit up further. "Baby…"

"No," she grits out. "I know you were drunk, and maybe you really don't remember. But that doesn't excuse anything, Everett. That doesn't make everything just automatically forgivable."

"I know. I'm not trying to use it as an excuse, I just…"

"I know. You love me." She says as if to say, *"so you've said before."*

"Yes." I nod. "It took us how long to get here? I just…can't we start over?"

"Start over? Where, fourth grade? Trust me if you were *any* other guy in the world, I wouldn't even be giving you a second thought. Our history is the *only* thing in your favor right now."

"Well, that should mean something, right? You know me, you know this isn't me. I don't cheat…" I pause because I have cheated on more than one occasion and on different girls. "I would never cheat on *you*."

"You did." *Fuck.* "Maybe you didn't fuck her, but something *happened* in that bed and it's not fair for you to think I should just get over it like that." She snaps. "Just because you were drunk and don't remember. I have to hold you accountable for your actions, Everett."

This is it.

This is the end of eleven years of friendship. I ruined eleven years in one stupid drunken night I have no recollection of.

"Leigh…"

"I'm not saying this is the end. I just asked for space and you bulldozed over me and touched me and kissed me and brought me home and…I need to think."

My palms begin to sweat, and my throat feels drier than a summer day in Phoenix. "Think about what? Me? What's there to think about? If you can forgive me?"

"I've forgiven you, Everett. It's not about that." She shakes her head and holds her wrist up to reveal her half of our tattoo. "This means I'll always forgive you." I'm off the bed and moving across the room towards her but she puts her hands up which stops me in my tracks. "But that doesn't mean I think we should be together. It doesn't mean that I trust you enough to give you my heart."

"Leigh, I've had your heart, for longer than we both realize."

She swallows and twists her lips into a frown that makes me feel like my world is crashing down around me. "It kinda feels like you gave it back."

Five

Leighton

You did this.
 You asked for space.
 You told him not to contact you.

I didn't expect him to listen! My mind argues as I walk across campus towards my eleven-thirty class. Usually Everett walks with me since our classes are in adjacent buildings, but now, as I scan the quad for him, I don't see him anywhere.

Is he skipping?

My fingers itch to text him to ask him if he's going to class when I spot him on the other side of the quad. He's walking pretty much in line with me but at least fifty yards away. His hood is pulled up, but I can tell by his walk, by his stature, everything screams the man I've loved since I was nine years old. He's by himself, and I resist the urge to cut across the grassy field between us so we can walk together, but I ignore the impulse and continue walking on my side. I cast another glance at him and I can tell he's looking right at me. I can feel my heart in my throat before I turn my head forward and continue my trek. The wind whips around me and I pull my jacket tighter around me as I make my way up the steps of the gray brick finance building. I turn my head one final time and watch as he enters the building without a glance in my direction.

I turn my key in the lock to my townhouse, and I'm met with a bare-naked ass as soon as I step into the living room. "Oh, for the love of God!" I shriek just as I watch Skyler's ex-professor plow into her. "Do I need to see this right now?" I put my hand over my eyes.

Do I care that I just walked in on my roommate and her boyfriend fucking? No, not really. Am I annoyed that I had to witness someone having sex when I'm currently going through 'sex with Everett' withdrawals?

Yep.

"Oh fuck!" Skyler shrieks as Aidan scrambles off of her.

"Don't you have an apartment of your own to do this at? One *without* roommates?" I look at her much older boyfriend before shutting my eyes. Aidan now teaches at Brookfield School of Law on the other side of town, which could be at least a forty minute drive at this hour with traffic, which means he must not have class today.

"Shit, why aren't you in class!" I hear her shriek. I open my eyes just as they both pull their clothes on.

"I'm skipping, and spare me the lecture, Professor." I nod at Aidan. "By the way, nice ass." I raise an eyebrow at him and watch as the pink floods his cheeks under his stubble. I trudge out of the room towards the kitchen to hear Skyler right behind me.

"I'm so sorry. I wasn't expecting you home and… I have office hours at four. Aidan just surprised me…shit. Should I tell him to go?"

"No, Sky, it's fine. I don't care." I wave at her. "It's your house too, and your couch if we are getting technical." Skyler comes from money, quite frankly a ton of money, which is why our townhouse is furnished with the swankiest shit and not a thing from Ikea. I swear the Mitchells have stock in *West Elm*.

"I know, but I...I don't want you to be uncomfortable," she whispers.

"About seeing *your* boyfriend's ass? Sky, I'll live."

"Okay, I'll leave like a sock or something on the door next time." She giggles, and just like that she's made me feel a fraction better. Skyler has a good heart and the cheeriest disposition all. the. time. It would be irritating as fuck if she wasn't such a goddamn sweetheart. She's been my rock the past week and has basically told Aidan to stay away to be at my beck and call. Hell, I didn't blame her for trying to squeeze in a quickie. And I certainly didn't blame Aidan for showing up and attempting to take his girlfriend back from her needy roommate. Aidan worships that girl like he doesn't have any sense.

Sound familiar? My heart thumps.

"That'd be great." I give her a thumbs up.

"What's up with you ditching anyway?" She hops up on the counter and begins to swing her feet as I make myself a sandwich.

"I couldn't focus and today's class was optional," I tell her.

She cocks her head to the side and gives me a look that makes me want to cry. *I can't handle Skyler's pity.* Even if she wouldn't call it pity, I know she feels what I'm going through. "Did...did you see Everett?"

"Walking to Financial Analysis, yeah." I lean over the counter and rest my head on my forearms.

"Did he see you?"

"I think so," I say without looking up.

"Have you guys still not talked?"

"Nope."

I sense movement in my peripheral vision and when I look up, Aidan is moving into the kitchen, the guilt over intruding written all over his face. "I'm sorry to interrupt. Baby, I have to go."

"Wait, now?" Her eyes widen as she hops off the counter and scurries across the room into his arms so fast it's like there's a magnetic pull between them.

"Yeah, I have a lecture at six." He leans down and rubs his nose against hers, and she frowns slightly.

"Wait…" She looks at me, and I put my hands up before I slip out of the room to give them some privacy. I hang outside of the kitchen because, evidently, I'm a glutton for punishment and I want to torment myself by witnessing how perfect Aidan and Skyler really are.

"I miss you," she tells him and I hear the sound of a slow kiss. "And we didn't finish." I frown as I suddenly feel like the worst roommate for cockblocking my girl from an orgasm.

"I know, I miss you too. My bed is fucking lonely without you. But your friend needs you. And I get that." The words go straight to my heart; Aidan really is a gem.

"But I need *you*. Will you come back later?"

"If I'm going to get lucky, maybe." She must give him a look because he chuckles. "I'm kidding. Of course, I've missed sharing a bed with you."

"I've missed waking up with your mouth between my legs."

Aaaaand that's my cue. I move up the stairs two at a time as quietly as I can, to not alert them that I was spying. When I open my door, my mouth drops open when I see what's on my bed. I swallow as I take in the bouquet of white roses and bring them slowly to my nose.

"He dropped them by a little before you got home." I hear Skyler's voice behind me and I turn around to see her giving me a sad smile. "He didn't look good, Leigh."

"Worse than me?"

"Way worse."

I wonder if she's just saying that because I didn't know it was possible that anyone could look worse than me right now. My hair looks like I haven't run a brush through it in days. I'm barely wearing makeup, and I'm on day three of wearing the same pair of leggings.

"I miss him. Does that make me pathetic?" I hate the way my voice sounds. I hate not being sure of myself. I hate everything about this.

"No!" She rushes through the room and engulfs me in a hug. She's at least three inches shorter than me, making it so her head rested right under my chin. She pulls back and looks up at me. "I would never call you pathetic. This whole thing with Everett is so…gray."

I shoot her a look. "No, it's not."

"Yes, babe, it is. Do I think the situation sucks? Yes. Do I think he's in the wrong? Also, yes. He shouldn't have allowed himself to get in that situation. I completely cosign that. But… were you guys technically together? He was *still* with Alli, if you want to be real."

"Really?"

"Leigh, Everett has proved that the only person his loyalty lies with is you. Who hasn't done stupid shit when they've been fucked up?"

"So, we're just allowing it then? So, if he were Aidan, you'd forgive him?"

She bites her bottom lip. "It's different."

"How? Because I've known Everett eleven years and you've known Aidan eleven *months*?"

She continues to chew her bottom lip, and I instantly feel like shit for talking to her like that. "Don't take this shit out on me, Leigh. All I'm saying is it's complicated. If it wasn't you wouldn't be hurting this much." I look at the roses on my bed and run my finger over one of the petals. "Go see him, Leigh. Stop being so fucking stubborn. Or you can waste ten years and then one day he'll confess his love for you just as you board a flight to Paris for a new job, and you'll have to get off the plane because you realize you've been stupid this whole time and you love him too." She blinks at me as a smile finds her lips.

I blink my eyes several times at her. "Did you just compare us to Ross and Rachel from FRIENDS?"

"Maybe."

"So, you agree they weren't on a break then?" I raise an eyebrow at her. It's a back and forth we have every time we watch that season. I believe they weren't on a break, and Skyler, ever the law student, sees both sides—and sometimes sided with God awful Ross.

"No, Rachel's an asshole. I mean to be fair, so are you. Look, you get what I'm saying!" She puts her hands on her hips. "Go talk to him." I nod and let out a breath as I grab my keys and head towards the door when I hear Skyler say my name. "Uhhh, girl you may wanna shower first."

I'm freshly showered, shaved, exfoliated, and I feel like my old self again. My hair has its luster back, which is currently sporting loose waves that cascade down my back. I'm wearing a pair of *clean* leggings underneath a long v-neck sweater that shows more than a hint of cleavage under a leather jacket. I've put on makeup and perfume and jewelry but quite frankly I don't know why I did all of this when I'm not even sure what I want.

Because you were thinking with your freshly shaved vagina.

I roll my eyes at my subconscious as I knock on his door later that night. I see the lights flickering in his living room making me believe they're all home which unfortunately means, we'll probably have an audience. I go to knock again when Pat and Dave answer the door together, and I resist the urge to make a sarcastic joke. My eyes flit back and forth between them as they step onto the porch and close the door behind them.

"Uhh…what?" I ask wondering why they seem to be skeptical about letting me inside.

"What's up, Leigh?" Dave asks and I frown. Pat crosses his arms in front of his chest as he sizes me up. *What is this good cop, bad cop routine?*

"Not much, is Everett here?"

Dave and Pat exchange a look before Pat speaks up. "Why?"

"Why what?" I ask.

"Why are you here? Because quite frankly Everett can't take much more, so if you're here to yell at him or tell him he ain't shit, then as much as I like you, you're going to have to go."

I blink my eyes several times like I wasn't just asked to leave. "Excuse me?"

"Dave's right. He's…not doing well, and you coming over here looking like…that," he waves his hand up and down my body, "will probably kill him when you tear his heart out *again*."

"Why are you talking to me like *I* did something wrong?"

Dave puts his hands up in defense. "We're not, but he already feels bad enough. Why are you beating a dead horse? You don't want anything to do with him, so why are you here?"

I'm just about to tell them both off for their fucking attitudes even if I do admire them for sticking up for Everett, when the door opens behind them.

"What the hell is going on?" He looks from Dave to Pat to me and I take a second to look him over. Skyler was right, he does look like he's been going through it. His facial hair had grown in a little more, which only successfully turns me into a horny mess. His hair is sticking up in a bunch of different directions and his eyes are a dull lifeless blue with bags underneath them. Now that he isn't in his usual hoodie, hiding his physique from the world, I can see that he's lost some weight but he's bulked up in his arms. *Fuck, he still looks good.*

"Nothing..." Dave shrugs as he slides past him and back into the house, leaving us alone with Pat.

"Get lost," he growls at Pat who rolls his eyes. He shoots me a look from behind Everett's back before he closes the door.

"Hey."

"Hi."

"You look nice..." he tells me.

"Thank you. Can...can I come in? It's kind of cold out here." I pull my jacket tighter around me. *Why am I so nervous? I'm never nervous around Everett.*

His eyes widen, assumedly at my expression of discomfort. "Of course, come on in." He opens the door for me, and I walk through to see Dave and Pat watching television on the couch. They narrow their gazes at me, and Everett must catch them because he snaps, "You got a problem?"

They both give him their middle fingers and he ushers me into the kitchen. "Are you hungry or thirsty?" he asks me as he leans against the counter.

"No. Do we have to be here? I mean…maybe we should go to your room?" His eyebrows go up to his hairline. "I just mean…for privacy?"

"Yeah, come on," he tells me, and I follow him up the stairs.

The second he closes the door behind us it feels like time stands still. I don't miss the way his eyes roam over my body, and I can't stop *my* body's reaction to it. "Are you going somewhere?"

I look down and shake my head. "No…well, I was thinking about going to the library later."

He clears his throat and looks out the window of his bedroom. A tree sits outside his window blocking the view of the last few moments of sun. "By yourself? Or is Sky going with you? Or are you, you know, just…walking around by yourself at night?" *He's nervous, and holy fuck is it cute.* Under normal circumstances, the Everett Cartwright I know would be telling me that there is no fucking way I'm going to the library at night alone.

"Or…or maybe you could come with me?" I fiddle with my purse as my eyes search his face for any signs that maybe he'd lost interest in *us*.

But his eyes are light, and I see the smile in them before the one tugging at his lips. "I have a paper due Monday."

"Have you started?"

He looks off to the side and blanches slightly. "I've had a lot on my mind."

"Me too," I tell him honestly. He doesn't say anything, so I continue. "Listen, Everett…I miss you." I shake my head as the tears well in my eyes. "All the time. There's been no less than a hundred things just *today* I've wanted to text you about." I take a step towards him and he closes the gap, putting us toe to toe. "I'm scared," I tell him. "I'm scared that we won't be *us* after this and…losing us would change me, Everett. It would be one of those instances that I'd look back on at the end of my life and think, that's where my life changed. That's where *I* changed." I take a deep breath. "*We* wouldn't survive breaking up…" I chuckle. "If girls were meant to date their best friend, I would be dating Skyler."

His eyes light up and he raises an eyebrow. "Can I watch?" I shoot him a mocking glare and push his shoulder. He catches my arm with one and wraps his other arm around me. He leans down, running his nose down my face and I hear him inhale my skin. "God, I've missed you. I'm so fucking sorry, baby. For everything. Just know, that I'm never giving you up." He pulls back and his blue eyes are burning with fire and my sex immediately reacts to it. A tingle ignites between my legs and I instantly press them together in an attempt to quell the sensation.

"Promise?" That wasn't what I intended to say, but it slips out on its own.

He nods before his hands slide up my arms and to my neck, before sliding up my face and into my hair. He rubs my scalp gently, knowing how much I love that, *especially when we're in the shower,* and I moan under his fingertips. "We do this, Leighton. You need to be all in. You can't run from me at the first sign of trouble."

"I didn't run…"

"You shut me out all week."

We are not off to a good start. I take a step back. "Should we rehash *why* I felt the need to put space between us?"

He takes a step closer. "No." He shakes his head. "We don't. But I don't ever intend to be in a situation like that."

"Well, I won't feel the need to shut you out then. I was all in last week, Everett."

He nods in understanding. "I'm all in, Leigh. You. Me. Us. *This.*"

I bite my bottom lip wondering if he's planning to seal that with a kiss, but he sits on his bed and holds his hand out for me. When I'm within arm's reach, he pulls me onto his lap and submerges his face in my neck. "I love you." I hum in response, letting my eyes flutter closed as his nose finds my pulse point and his tongue darts out to lick the skin. "Tell me, did you miss me, baby? Did you rub your sweet little pussy because I wasn't around to make you scream?"

"Fuck." I let out a breath. "Everett..." His hand drags up my leg and settles at the apex of my thighs rubbing his fingers against the seam right over my pussy. My leggings aren't particularly thin, but enough so that I can feel the pressure on my clit, *easily*.

I feel his breath on my face. "That feel good?" My eyes shut the second he started rubbing me and when they flutter open, his piercing blue eyes are staring right at me. "Making you come is high on my list of favorite pastimes, and I haven't done that in what feels like forever. Please, let me."

I believe that. When Everett and I first started messing around all those years ago, the first time he made me come, you'd think someone would have crowned him king of the fucking world. He didn't shut up for *days* about it. Not to anyone else or anything, but he was so proud of the fact that he got me off.

And to be honest, so was I. A few of my friends were starting to lose their v-cards around the same time and none of them knew what an orgasm felt like. I did, and I was having them daily.

"Everett…" I grab his hand despite the dizzy feeling and lean forward to press my forehead to his. "I just…I think we should take this a little slower…"

"Last time you said that, you ran," he whispers.

"I know, but I'm sober, and I'm telling you I want this, but I don't want to jump back into bed yet. We know we have this insane sexual chemistry. That will never change, but I need to know that I'm in love with more than just our sex life. I need to know that I love you as more than just my best friend. We need to…" I look around the room as I struggle to explain what I mean, *"date."*

"Okay…" He trails off. "But people fuck when they're dating usually." He narrows his eyes, confused.

"Yes, but not usually, night one. Okay, sometimes night one, but…ugh…" I scoff when I see the grin on his lips. "Everett, you get what I'm saying."

"I do. We'll keep things PG for now." He wraps his arms around me completely and presses a kiss to my shoulder.

Wait, let's not get crazy! I still want to make out. "Whoa whoa whoa." I put a hand up. "What's PG?"

"Like making out?"

"That's not PG. A kiss maybe, but I don't think there's tongue till PG-13." I tap my chin as I try to recall some tween movies.

"Sex is PG-13, babe."

Okay, he's got a point. "Well…what about PG-13 with no sex?"

His eyes widen. "What kind of bullshit movie is that?"

"I don't know…a fade to black one? All sex behind closed doors? I don't know."

"So, I don't see your tits?"

"You've seen my tits, Everett."

"Not *today*. I feel like it's been forever. Did you have them pierced? Did they grow?" he jokes.

I roll my eyes at my dramatic best friend…*boyfriend…best friend slash boyfriend*. "They look the same."

"I'll be the judge of that." He tells me as he pulls my sweater slightly forward so he can peer down my shirt and I shiver when he licks his lips. "Still beautiful," he mumbles.

"Okay, so library?" *If we don't get out of here, we're going to have sex. I'm already two seconds from ripping my clothes off and sitting on his face.*

"Yeah, if I'm in here another minute with you, I'm going to lose my fucking mind."

Six

Leighton

"Everett…" I can't stop the giggle from escaping my lips as his mouth trails kisses up and down my neck.

"What?" he mumbles against my skin, and I feel his teeth grazing my pulse point that's flickering with desire in my neck.

I pull back slightly and look around the private study room he all but insisted on us getting. *Now I see why.* The small study space is no bigger than my bedroom and Everett has basically been on top of me since we walked in. "Didn't I say I needed to *study*? And aren't we taking things slow?"

"We are! If we weren't, my mouth would be on your pussy and not your neck." He tugs my hair slightly and my sex clenches.

Fuck. Pull my hair again.

"Everett…" I turn my face to look at him and my nose grazes his lip gently. I run my tongue over my bottom lip and his hands are on my face instantly, running his thumb over the trail my tongue made.

"I missed you so much." His voice is hoarse and low and it speaks to me on the most primal level. It washes over me like a warm summer rain. Seductive and erotic and making my skin tingle.

Holy shit, is he seducing me?

Whatever he's doing, I want it. I want his lips on mine. I wanted his body rubbing against mine. I wanted every bit of him he's offering up to me on a silver platter.

My eyes trace over his features and land on his lips. "Kiss me."

His lips turn up slightly before he presses his mouth to mine. His tongue slides into my mouth and just like that, I'm home. He tastes familiar. Like comfort. Like home.

He'll always be home.

The first two weeks of freshman year, I was so homesick. I missed my parents and my bed and my cat. I even missed my annoying little brother. All I wanted was to curl up in my mom's arms. If it hadn't been for Everett basically rocking me to sleep every night, I would have been on the first flight back to Arizona.

Everett is my security blanket. He's always made me feel safe and protected. Ever since I was nine years old.

Why am I fighting the thought that he could be more?

He pulls back and cocks his head to the side. "I can hear you thinking."

"No, you can't."

"You forget we practically share a brain."

"Oh really? Then what am I thinking now? And more importantly, why am I not doing better in stats?" I raise an eyebrow at him and he shakes his head.

"You're thinking...*why did I say we should take things slow? And why did this asshole put on gray sweatpants? Little slut.*"

My mouth drops open at his perfect impersonation of me. "I...why *are* you in gray sweatpants?" My eyes drop to his crotch on their own and then back up to his eyes that seem to be answering my question all on their own.

"I don't know what you're talking about?" He smiles and I turn back to my textbook.

"Don't touch me, you're trying to break me, and I am trying to be strong."

I meant it as a joke, and I assumed he'd say something snarky in response, but the silence washes over the room instantly. I turn my gaze towards him, and his blue eyes are sad and full of shame and regret. "I would never *try* to break you. I know I fucked up and—"

"Wait wait wait, I was kidding! That's not where I was going with that! Weren't we just making out?" I lean forward to continue, and he pulls away and shakes his head much to my surprise.

"I know…I just…you asked me not to break you and then I did, so I guess that word just… triggered me a little."

"Oh." I let out a small puff of air before turning back to my book. "Sorry."

He grabs my hand and pulls it into his, pressing a small kiss to the skin. I take a second to grasp his clean shaven jaw. He rarely sports any facial hair, and he's asked me literally a million times over the years if I think he looks hotter with a beard. I always thought he was just being vain, but maybe he just wanted to look *good for me*. He wanted *me* to find him attractive. The thought hits me like a ton of bricks as I look over the man that I believed could get any girl he wanted.

But all this time he's only wanted me.

"Leighton." My eyes dart up from his jaw to meet his and I'm captivated by their color as I move into his lap to straddle him. I slide my hands up his chest to his shoulders and grind my pelvis down on him. His thick cock jerks underneath me and he stills my hips. "Is this taking it slow?" He tightens his grip and I shiver under the delicious pain shooting through me.

I move again, despite the grip he has on me and shoot him a wicked grin. "Maybe a little faster than slow." I wanted more and harder and faster. I know I need to make sure my heart is ready before I open my legs again but I'm crumbling under his gaze and gentle touches and sexy words. He has a power over my mind and body and heart that not only makes me feel alive but also scares the shit out of me. *But I thrive on it.*

I press my lips to his and slide my tongue into his mouth as I begin to rub against him, riding him through our clothes like I would his dick. He pulls away, grabbing a fistful of my hair and latching onto my neck, teeth first. "Oh fuck," I moan. "Oh God, Everett!" I'm trying to keep my voice down as to not alert the entire third floor of the library what's going on in this study room, but I *almost* don't care.

His hand moves underneath my sweater and squeezes my breast through my bra. "Fuck, you drive me so crazy," he murmurs against my skin. His lips are still sucking at my neck and I don't need a mirror to know there's a significant bruise forming on my skin.

I'm still rubbing against him, his cock hard and wanting beneath me. He jerks upwards into me just as I grind down and we groan in unison. "You're going to come, aren't you?" he grits out, before tugging my head back to look in my eyes. His eyes are dark and full of hunger that I can feel in my clit which pulses every time he blinks.

My panties are soaked and wedged between my lips from riding him so hard making the pleasure so intense it's almost uncomfortable. My whole body is tightening, like a coil prepared to snap, and I feel the air leaving my lungs with each passing second.

"Tell me you love me first." His eyes are trained on me, his heart open and exposed as we both prepare to fall over the edge. "Before you even think of coming, I want you to look me in the eyes and tell me you love me. That you belong to me. That you want *this* as bad as I do. You're guarded, I can tell. Let it down, baby, I need us to be *us*."

I shake in his arms, trying to hold off the orgasm that is no more than a beat away. He lifts me up by my arms and off of his dick and holds me there. My clit tingles as the heady feelings float away. "No! Everett!" I cry out as I try to get back into his lap.

"Tell me," he demands.

"You know I do," I cry. Actually cry. The tears spring to my eyes at the pain of being so wound up without release. "This isn't fair."

"Say it, Leigh. Say it and I'll let your pretty pussy cream all over my lap."

I snap. "I love you, all right!" I grip his jaw, tears threatening to fall down my cheeks by how worked up I am in every way. "I love you so much, you possessive asshole! I want this, but I swear on all that's holy, I'll rip your dick off if you hurt me again."

He smiles. "There's my girl." He lets me go and I fall into his lap again. He grips my hips and our lips violently crash as we rub against each other. Harder and faster with every stroke. His teeth bite my bottom lip, sucking it into his mouth and I moan. "Come for me, baby."

My long lost orgasm is back instantly, as if it's returning in response to his command. I shudder in his arms as my body succumbs to the pleasure, digging my nails into his shoulder as I float back to Earth. "You're going to destroy my back later, aren't you?" he growls in my ear.

Everett and I both have a thing for marking the other, especially when we've been without each other for an extended period of time. It goes hand in hand with wanting his hands around my throat. With pulling my hair and biting my skin. It's rare that Everett's back isn't scratched beyond belief after a particularly rough session. Once in high school, I went away to soccer camp for a month and within two hours of being back home, Everett had scratches down his back like a cat had attacked him.

I'm about to respond to him when there's a knock on the study room door and our eyes snap towards the noise. "If you're not actually studying, can you come out? Go somewhere else and do that." A guy that sounds like his balls haven't dropped, much less hit puberty commands from the other side. "I'm going to open the door."

"You'll regret it," Everett booms, and I bite my lip as the tingles return at his alpha-like comment.

"Let's just go, I'm hungry anyway," I whisper.

His eyes snap to mine with a glint in them. *"For...me?"*

"No, for food." I roll my eyes.

"And maybe also me?"

"You wish." I give him a pointed glare as I get off his lap, knowing that *he* didn't come but I certainly did. I shoot him a look filled with mischief. "Did you think I was going to make it that easy for you?"

The smell of maple syrup fills the air as I place pancakes on our plates. Despite the fact that it is well past ten PM, I had a craving for breakfast. I'm surprised I haven't burned my house down with the way Everett is distracting me. He stands directly behind me almost the entire time, his erection digging into my back and his lips on my neck. At one point he'd slid his hand between my legs and rubbed me gently while I whisked the batter.

Now we are sitting at my dining room table feeding each other pancakes when he misses my mouth smearing maple syrup into my skin. "Hey!" I giggle.

"Oh shit, let me get that." He smiles and presses his lips to the sticky skin, swiping his tongue across my chin and cheek to collect the sweet syrup. "You make the syrup taste sweeter."

This man is wearing me down slowly but surely.

I'm leaning in to kiss him when his phone, which is sitting on the table between us, begins to ring. I catch a look at the name and then up at him questioningly.

"Why is Alli calling?" *I don't think Everett is doing anything shady, necessarily, but I'm irritated that he hasn't made it clear not to contact him.*

"I don't know. I... I'm not going to answer it."

Envy slithers up my spine and grips my brain, and I wouldn't be surprised if I was turning greener by the second. "Has she been calling?" I blurt out.

"No. Maybe once since I broke up with her." *Bitch*

"Have you seen her?" *Okay, Leigh, rein in the crazy.*

Everett already knows you're crazy. I argue with myself. *What's the use in hiding it?*

"Leigh…" He rubs his hand down my arm and clasps our hands.

I slide my hand out of his grasp and cross my arms. "Have you seen her? It's a simple question, Everett."

"No, I haven't and I don't want you getting up in arms about her. She means nothing."

"She meant enough for you to date her." I argue, petulantly.

"Leighton," he growls.

"Why are you scolding me for being upset?"

"I'm not, baby. I just…hate that you're upset." I look in his warm eyes, filled with kindness and regret and love and hurt. Eyes that I know are full of truth. "And I hate myself for doing this to you." He looks away from me and towards the front door of my townhouse. He shakes his head. "I just want to make you happy," he mumbles. "Why is that so fucking hard?" His words successfully knock the wind out of me. My chest tightens and for a second, I feel like my heart might explode from my chest. Everett Cartwright does make me happy. Ever since we were nine years old, when I linked our pinkies and told him we were best friends. Things weren't so complicated then. Happiness was such a simple concept. A simplicity I long for as we take our relationship into uncharted territory.

"You do." I bite my lip and move across the table to sit in his lap in an attempt to lighten the mood. I rub my nose against his, and a smile floats across his face. "Sorry," I whisper, "for being crazy."

He raises an eyebrow at me and pinches my side playfully. "I like you a little bit crazy."

I slam my hand down on the bed, as my face is pushed hard into the mattress. "HARDER!" I screech as Everett plows into me from behind. One hand is in my hair, pulling hard as he simultaneously pushes me down, and I feel my pussy start to pulse in preparation for the orgasm I know is only moments away. "Stay the fuck down, Mills," he growls as he lets my face go and lays a hard smack to my ass.

Fuck. Again. Please!

"You want more?" he asks and I wonder if I spoke aloud or if he really can hear my thoughts.

"Yes! More!"

"Ask me nicely."

"No," I sass and begin to salivate for his response to my comment. I bite my bottom lip, preparing for his reaction when I feel his nails dig into my ass. I yelp and curl my toes as the delicious pain takes over. "Please."

The "taking things slow" idea had long been forgotten the second we were alone in my bedroom. It only took one look for our clothes to start flying and his cock to slide down my throat.

I shiver as his thick cock stretches me. He fucks me so hard; I swear I can feel his dick in my soul. *But I need more*. My hand immediately goes between my legs and I graze his cock as he goes in and out of me. I rub my clit, desperate for more friction in between thrusts when his balls slap against my sex. His hands tighten on my hips and then suddenly I feel empty. My sex immediately feels cold without his dick inside of me warming my insides.

I frown. "What are you doing?" He flips me over on my back and stares down at me. "Did I say you could touch it?" He strokes his dick from root to tip, rubbing the juices from my sex all over it. We'd forgone condoms this time in a haste for him to get inside of me, and I clench at the sexiness of it.

"I was close…"

"And?" He raises an eyebrow at me. "If you want to come, I'll take care of it if you ask nicely."

"Screw you," I spit out before sinking my teeth into my bottom lip in attempts to rile him up.

He clicks his tongue against his teeth before he leans forward tickling my clit with the tip of his hard cock. A creamy bead forms at the head and I watch as he wipes it against my slit. He spreads my lips open and I whimper as the air hits my wet cunt. "It's my job to make you come, Leighton." He leans down and hovers above me, his dick rubbing against my pelvis. I try to arch myself to get him inside of me, but it's no use as it tickles the area around my navel. "And I take my job very seriously," he whispers against my lips before letting his tongue dart out to lick them.

He trails his tongue down my body, stopping at my right nipple. He sucks it into his mouth, nibbling gently on the sensitive nub that always has me crying out. Everett loves biting me everywhere, but there is something about my nipples that makes him more aggressive. He bites harder there than anywhere else and it always causes a reaction somewhere between crying out in pleasure and in pain. The line is faint, but I loved searching for it.

He bites a little harder every few seconds and I already feel the indents in my skin from his teeth marks forming. He lets me go with a pop. "It's been over a week since I've licked your pussy."

"Trust me, I know." I swallow in preparation for his mouth between my thighs. I love everything about the rough sex, the aggression, the roles of dominant and submissive we take on in the bedroom because they are so different from our everyday life. But when his mouth is on me, *there*, he is just *Everett*. The nervous young guy that turned beet red the first time he asked if he could taste me. The young boy that got teased for having a girl best friend. The man I'm madly in love with.

In those moments, he isn't aggressive. He doesn't bite

or spank or pull. He worships and loves and turns me inside out in soft, warm strokes. His tongue is strong and unrelenting, but it's soft and sweet as he makes love to me. It's like his tongue is telling me he loves me in a voice only my pussy can understand.

It's insane.

"Fuck," he whispers, I think to himself because I barely hear him over my heavy breathing. "I'll never not want this." He presses his lips to my sex and slides his tongue through my folds.

"Oh my God." My eyes immediately flutter closed as I feel my body begin to build.

"Look at me, baby," he tells me, though his words are muffled as his tongue hasn't moved from my clit. I look down at him and almost come right then and there when I see my cum on his tongue, mixing with his spit. I used to be embarrassed at how wet I could get, but Everett successfully fucked all of the humiliation out of me years ago. Now, I attempt to drown him every time we fuck.

He slides two fingers inside of me and curls them upward and I curl my toes into the mattress. "Everett!"

"You know what I want."

Everett's favorite thing is to make me squirt, and although I can't every time, sometimes he can force my body into it if I'm just close enough to the edge while we're in this position. I nod as I feel myself falling over the edge. "Oh my God, I'm coming." I grab his head, holding him in place, our eyes locked in this intimate moment and right on cue the words leave my lips. "I love you so fucking much." The tears spring to my eyes, and I try to move up the bed away from his mouth but he moves with me, pinning my legs down and keeping his mouth attached to me as a rush of fluid flies from my sex.

"Yes, yes fucking *yes*," he growls like he's a man in a desert that just found water. He drinks from me like he'd been parched forever, lapping at the space between my legs as if I'm a fountain.

When I finally float back down to Earth, my arms and legs feel boneless and all I want is to snuggle in Everett's arms and go to sleep.

"So that's two orgasms for Princess Leighton."

"No one told you to pull out." I yawn and let my eyes flutter closed. "You knew what you were doing and once you make me squirt it's game over."

He chuckles and I feel him push my wet hair from my face. He presses a kiss to my forehead, and then I'm moving slowly into his arms and thankfully out of the puddle I made on my bed. He pulls the blanket up over us and kisses my nose one final time. "I love you."

I press my lips to his bare chest and nod. "We can fuck when I wake up."

"You bet your ass we will." His voice is even and quiet. "And I do quite literally mean *your ass*."

Seven

Everett

I'T'S BEEN QUITE POSSIBLY THE BEST THREE WEEKS OF MY LIFE. Sure, I've always enjoyed my time with Leighton, but there's something so different about us now.

She's really mine now.

And fuck if I don't love being hers.

Especially every morning with her special wake up calls.

Dave and Pat finally stopped ragging on me for being pussy whipped because they realized I could not give less of a fuck what their single asses thought. I have Leighton. The girl I've been in love with for as long as I can remember.

School is great. I'm still on track to graduate summa cum laude, we're undefeated in lacrosse, and I'm spending every night inside of my favorite person in the world. And the sex... sex I thought was already fucking mind blowing, somehow *got better*.

Nothing can bring me down.

I'm sitting on the quad on the first truly warm day of the year when I feel hands over my eyes and a wet kiss on my cheek. "Guess who?"

"Umm...Skyler?" I joke

"Fuck off." She scoffs as she plops her pert little ass into my lap and moves around far too much.

"Shit, baby, can you not?" I grip her hips to stop her from moving when she looks up at me with those deviously sexy eyes.

"I'm horny as fuck, can we go home *pleeeease*?" she whines. I push her cheeks together and press my lips to hers.

"I need to stop by one of my professor's office hours but meet you at my car in like twenty?" I look down at my watch before meeting her gaze.

"Okay, I'm going to grab some sodas from the dining center. I think we're out of chasers and I don't feel like going to the grocery store."

It's *Thirsty Thursday* and the first one after a hellish midterm week, so a bunch of us are looking to cut loose. I don't have class on Fridays, and Leighton's class was canceled, so we are already preparing to do some serious damage to our livers tonight.

"Okay, but can you get something *besides* diet?" I give her a pointed look and she runs her tongue up her middle finger lasciviously before blowing me a kiss.

Little tease.

I'm leaning against my car waiting for Leighton when I notice movement out of the corner of my eye. "Baby, I—" I look up from my phone expecting it to be Leighton with two bottles of diet coke just to spite me when Alli comes into view. Her face is pale and she's barely wearing a stitch of makeup, which is unlike her.

"Hey, Everett." Her voice is quiet and unsure, and I'm immediately on the defense that she's about to hand me a sob story about how I hurt her and she wants me back.

"Alli..." I immediately search the perimeter of the parking lot for Leighton. I'm not sure she'd lose it over us talking, but I couldn't be one hundred percent sure. "Ummm...how ya been?" I ask, trying my best to keep things light. I know I don't owe Alli anything necessarily, but as everyone has so eloquently put it, I did kind of fuck her over.

She lets out a breath and squeezes her eyes shut. "Pregnant."

I blink my eyes several times at her as she slowly opens hers. "What?"

"I'm pregnant, Everett. And before you get all twitchy and weird and dismissive, it's *yours*."

There are a million thoughts going through my head right now and none of them seem appropriate to blurt out at this moment, so I go with the least offensive. "What?"

The tears flood her blue eyes and she shakes them away. "My pill must have failed. I don't know...and..."

I put my hands up, but why? I don't know. Maybe to get her to stop talking or to prevent her from taking a step closer or maybe because I'm desperate for her to take *those* words back. "We didn't have sex, Alli," I interrupt.

"Still holding onto that, huh?" she snaps, her blue eyes angry and harsh.

"I wouldn't have fucked you without a condom."

"Even if we used one, they're not 100% effective, *bio major*." The sarcasm drips from her voice.

"It's too soon for you to know if—" I start doing some math in my head when she interrupts.

"Four weeks. I was late. I just left the health center...I was going to ask if we could meet up and then I saw you here... alone...without your shadow." My eyes snap to hers, warning her when she puts her hands up. "Look, I'm not trying to wreck things with your precious Leighton." *Nope, I'm going to do that all on my own.* My heart flips hearing her name fall from Alli's lips. *Leighton is going to hate me. She's going to leave me... fuck. Fuck. fuck.* "But—"

"Are you keeping it? I mean I support...but...you can't be, right?" I stumble over my words, not wanting to sound like some patriarchal asshole who doesn't believe in giving women choices. I shake my head, deciding to take a different approach. "You want to be cheer captain, and you do like a fuck ton of shit. You soak your liver in vodka three times a week. You want to be Beta Sig president, how are you going to do all of that with a fucking baby?"

She pulls at her ponytail and squeezes her eyes shut. "I don't...I don't know, Everett, but I don't think I could do *that*. It's...a baby."

"One you want to raise with me?" *This is bullshit and not how I imagined it would go the first time I was told I'd be a dad.*

First off, this is the wrong mom.

"Listen, I'm in just as much shock as you are. I just wanted to clue you in, I'm pregnant and...it's yours."

"You're a fucking liar." The words are higher than mine, although I may or may not have been thinking that at least a dozen times during this conversation. Leighton moves towards us, her hands shaking despite the bag of two-liters in her hands. I go to remove them from her grasp and although she flinches, she lets me take the heavy bags from her.

"I am not, Leighton," Alli spits out.

Leighton looks at me. The tears are there, but they haven't started sliding down her sweet face. "Tell me...tell me she's lying, Everett. *Please*," she pleads with me. *Actually pleads*. I've never known Leighton Mills to plead with me for anything except an orgasm. Her bottom lip trembles and just as I'm about to speak, Alli interjects.

"He *can't*. It's his baby. I haven't been with anyone since that night we slept together."

I can see that her words affect Leighton, although no one else could probably tell. She looks away from us both and I grit my teeth together, pissed that Leighton is suffering the brunt of this. "Alli, thanks for…telling me. Can we continue this conversation…" I look over at Leighton who looks like she's holding it together by a fucking thread, "later?"

"Of course. You have my number." She shoots a glare at Leighton, trying to dig the knife in deeper, I'm sure, but Leighton doesn't even seem to notice.

I have Leighton pinned against my car before she can decide that she doesn't want me to touch her. "Baby, say something."

"You're…you're going to have a baby?" She lets out a breath as the first of what I assume to be several tears start to fall. "With *her*? How? Why?" Her nostrils flare and she twists her lips into a pout that makes me believe she's chewing the inside of her cheek to keep from completely breaking down. I'm not sure if she was asking me those questions or the universe, but I'm quiet because quite frankly, I don't have the answers.

"It's funny," she continues. "I always…I always thought I'd be the mother when you decided to have a baby." She blinks the tears from her eyes and looks around the parking lot. I wrap my arms around her and she must be in shock because she snuggles her face against my chest.

"I want that…you and me having babies. I want that, sweetheart." I squeeze my eyes shut and curse every higher power for doing this to me. *I just want Leighton. All I fucking care about is Leighton, and this is going to ruin everything.*

"You slept with her, officially." She pulls back and scrunches her nose. "I was holding onto hope that you didn't."

"I still don't remember...I don't remember touching her. I..."

"Does that matter? The proof is in the pudding. Or...her womb...I don't know." She looks at me and makes her way to the other side of the car. "Can we go home? I want to start drinking. I'm getting absolutely hammered tonight."

"You did *what?*" Peyton's eyes are wide and like they're ready to kill. She slams her hand down on the counter next to the shots they'd poured and points at me. "I knew you were a shady fucking asshole," she growls and Skyler's eyes shoot to mine as if to say *I was on your side. I was rooting for you, but now...*

Leighton is sitting on the counter, eating pretzels directly out of a bag as she nurses what is quite possibly the largest glass of pure vodka, I've ever seen her ingest.

"Paternity...paternity tests. You can't be that dense that you're just taking her word for it. You guys have been apart for a month. And it's only that one time in question, right?" Skyler says as she looks back and forth between me and Leighton. I nod emphatically. "Let's just all relax." Skyler's eyes widen as she takes one of the shots Leighton poured. "She said that... like for real? A baby?"

I wasn't thrilled that Skyler and Peyton both learned the news before I had a real chance to talk to Leighton, but they were home and Leighton broke down within about a minute of her first shot which she took about two seconds after we walked through the door. I couldn't even blame her.

"Pregnant." Leighton points at me. "Baby daddy." She hiccups as she turns to me. "I really thought you didn't fuck her. I thought...I thought we'd both only ever be with each other forever." She looks down in her lap. "I guess that was just wishful thinking."

"It's not!" I urge as I move across the kitchen so that I'm standing in front of her. I lift her chin slightly to meet my gaze. "You're the only person I've ever…" I turn around and look at Skyler and Peyton. "Do you guys mind?"

"So, you can brainwash our friend? Uh uh." Peyton stamps her foot and I divert to Skyler hoping that she'll opt to give us some privacy and force Peyton out of the room, but she just stares at me with a solemn expression.

"I… I've always been on your side, Everett, but…Leigh?" She looks at Leighton and then at me before tucking a hair behind her ear.

"I'm not the only person you've ever…" Leighton whispers. "And now she's *pregnant*."

"Please don't run…please don't leave me."

"Oh, so this is all about you?" She narrows her gaze at me before snapping her eyes to her friends. "Out."

I almost want to turn around and beg her friends to stay, but now all of a sudden, they seem in a hurry to leave.

"Never mind this is the second time in a month you've shattered my heart into a million pieces. You're asking I don't leave you until when? You and Alli go play house in some sorority sponsored off campus housing? Pass." She snorts sarcastically but I can see the pain in her eyes.

"That's not going to happen, Leigh. At most, we'd learn to, I don't know, co-parent. But I'm never going to be with her. I want to be with you."

She nods her head. "Lucky me." She takes a large gulp of her drink and I wince. I want to take the drink from her, knowing nothing good would come from it, but I'm fairly certain that would be risking my life.

"Leighton…look at me," I command, and despite her devastation, her irritation, her anger, her eyes flit to mine. "I made a mistake. But you took me back knowing there was a chance I slept with her, and now it seems I did. And it's fucked up. You don't deserve this shit. But I love you. I love you more than I hate myself right now, and I know it's selfish, but I'm asking… *begging* that you just stick with me through this. I know this means Alli has to be in our lives, but I don't want her…there's no me and her. Only me and you."

Despite the fact that we were preparing to go out later, by five thirty Leighton is drunk, and I can see her shutting down in front of me. I'd foregone drinking for obvious reasons, so when she begins to stumble upstairs, I follow closely behind her to steady her if needed. I watch as she pulls her shoes off and lies on her bed. She stares at the ceiling for a few moments then squeezes her eyes shut and presses her face into the pillow. I watch as her shoulders begin to shake under the force of this shitty day.

"Baby…" I'm kneeling next to her bed in a second, rubbing her back and stroking her hair. "I'm so sorry. So fucking sorry."

When she turns to me her eyes are red and the space underneath them are already starting to swell slightly. "How… how could this happen? It's not fair."

"You're right, it's not fair. It's so fucking fucked up." I've been so focused on Leighton and how she's handling this that I don't think it hit me that I could potentially be a father in nine months. I let out a breath. "I'm not ready to be a father."

Her lip trembles and I want to rub my lips across hers to

try and take the pain away. "You're going to forget all about me."

"What?" I narrow my eyes at her. *Is she crazy? She's the center of my world. I'd never forget her.*

"You're going to have a baby and…I won't be important anymore."

"You'll always be important, Leigh. The most important."

"Not more important than your baby." She sighs. "Why couldn't it have been me?" she whimpers. "I would love your baby so much, Everett." Her eyes are glazed over and I'm not sure if it's all from the tears or from the alcohol hitting her hard and fast. She closes her eyes.

"I'd give anything for it to be you," I whisper as I take her hand in mine. I get up from next to her bed and crawl behind her, pulling her against my chest. I rub my knuckles down her face gently and she sighs as she succumbs to a liquor induced slumber. "Please don't give up on us, Leigh."

She turns around and snuggles face first into my chest, and I relish in her vulnerability.

She wants me to comfort her. She wants me to make this better. She doesn't hate me.

Yet.

Eight

Leighton

BEFORE I'M EVEN FULLY AWAKE, MY HEART SINKS IN MY chest. It sinks so far that I'm desperate to return to my prior comatose state so I don't have to deal with the shitstorm of my life.

Everett got Alli pregnant.
Everett is going to be a dad.
Everett is having a baby with someone else.

Nothing about this is fair and I have enough self-awareness to know that I'm going to have a difficult time coping with it. I'm not sure if I'm necessarily upset about the potential one-time incident where my man fucked another woman…although, that did really fucking piss me off.

But it's more than that. She's going to have him in a way I can't. A way I may never have him. And she's going to have him *forever*…or at the very least the next eighteen years. A very familiar lyric by Kanye West floats through my head and I remember Skyler's comment.

Could Alli be full of shit? Sure, she's petty and hates me, but would she really go this far? Faking a pregnancy? Or maybe she is, but it's not Everett's baby? Is this all a ploy so she can have him?

"I can hear you thinking." I'm brought into strong arms

and for a second I let them lull me into this false sense of security. For a second, I pretend that the beginnings of a tornado aren't swirling around us, threatening to tear up the solid foundation we've spent eleven years building. I turn in his arms and stare up into sleepy blue eyes.

"Can you blame me?" I whisper. His chest is bare and I press my face into the warm space just over his heart. There's a light smattering of hair but for the most part, he's pretty bare. He pulls me harder against him and I bump against his cock that's probably been up for longer than both of us have.

He pulls away slightly so that I'm not rubbing directly against it, and I can't decide if I'm relieved or annoyed. Physically, I'm ready to pounce. Mentally, I can't handle that level of intimacy while I'm combating an emotional hangover that rivals any physical one I've ever experienced. "What are you thinking about?" he asks.

"What happens now?"

"I don't know…" He pulls away from me to stare at my ceiling, and immediately I feel the absence of his touch. I know this situation is bigger than just my feelings, and I fear Everett will use that as a reason not to confide in me. He wouldn't risk upsetting me by disclosing his fears and I hate that.

I sit up and stare down at him. "Yes, you do," I murmur. "Talk to me. Don't shut me out, Everett. Not now."

He turns his head to look at me and reaches up to run a hand down my face. "This isn't your problem, and I hate that it's going to end up hurting you."

I furrow my brows and shake my head. "It's not a problem, Everett. It's a *baby*. And as much as I want to hate it… he, she, whatever…I can't. Because it's *your* baby. Even if it's not mine too. Don't hide things from me. I'm here. I want to be…I just…" I let out a breath. "It's just going to take some getting used to."

He nods and reaches up to pull me down by the back of my neck. "Thank you," he whispers. "I was worried I was going to have to do this without you."

*Well, you are…*my mind thinks involuntarily, and I slam my eyes shut at the thought. It's going to take some time to train my brain to not immediately revert to sarcasm or bitchy or anger with Everett—and even Alli. "I guess I should call my parents." He says.

"Eve and Mike are going to flip," I say. "No seriously, they're probably going to fly out here." I look up at the ceiling and a smile finds my face. "Actually, that wouldn't be the worst thing. I've been in the mood for a steak." Everett glares at me and I giggle. Despite their nasty divorce, they still show up for Everett. They had put on their polite faces and dealt with graduations and college move-in day three times and family weekends and championship lacrosse games. They donned their CGU parent gear and played nice for the weekend and it always ended up with a fancy dinner that I was always invited to. Sometimes Everett's stepdad would come, but Everett isn't too fond of him, so Eve kept his appearances to a minimum.

"My dad is going to kick my ass. He always warned me about wrapping it up." He groans. "Of course, he laid off when he figured out I was only banging you."

"As he should. He knows I'd give him some pretty as fuck grandchildren," I joke, and I realize that instead of sarcasm or anger, perhaps humor would be my go-to defense mechanism in all of this.

"*Will* give him some pretty as fuck grandchildren," Everett corrects.

I roll my eyes. "How about you focus on the one you've knocked up for now, okay?" *Ah, there's the sarcasm. Right on cue.* I'm off the bed and pulling on a pair of leggings and I can feel Everett's gaze following me around the room.

"Do you want me to go?" he asks, and I sigh, shaking my head.

"No…no I don't. If you leave, I'll just think you're with her and I'm just…I hate that you're going to have to spend time with her."

"Baby…" I can feel him preparing to placate me, and I don't want to hear it.

"No. I know it's stupid and silly, but I'm jealous, okay? I'm jealous and I hate that she wins." I run a brush through my hair and twist it into a bun at the top of my head.

"I don't think she wins, babe. Her whole life is about to be turned upside down."

"Are you defending her? She probably got pregnant on purpose," I snap as I pull Everett's t-shirt off and replace it with one of my own.

"Leigh…I doubt that." He snorts as he gets up, and I hate that he's dismissing my idea so quickly. He pulls on a pair of sweats and stands in front of me, putting his hands on my shoulders. "I get feeling jealous. And I can't blame you for feeling that way over the fact that there will be a baby, but I won't have you feeling jealous of Alli. If you're thinking she "won" me, then stop it. She didn't. I'm yours, Leigh." He says as his eyes bore into mine.

I sigh and nod slowly, trying to shake my insecurities from my brain with every nod of my head. We shuffle into the bathroom to brush our teeth and do other morning activities that have married couple written all over them before heading downstairs. When we get to the bottom, I see Peyton nursing a glass of orange juice that I'm sure is spiked with something as she scrolls through her phone. "Hey."

"Hey," Peyton looks me over and I can tell she's trying to read the situation as her eyes move back and forth between me and Everett.

"Where's Sky?"

"Upstairs sucking Aidan's dick, I'm assuming." She says as she turns back to her phone.

"A simple she's not up yet would have sufficed." I roll my eyes as I open the refrigerator, and sure enough, see a freshly popped bottle of champagne. She chuckles to herself and when I turn around, she downs the rest of her champagne. "Where's the fire?"

"I'm going to a day party at Alpha Pi." She's already dressed for the day, sporting her leather jacket and her favorite crop top with a pair of her *lucky* jeans. *And I don't mean the brand.*

"Alone?"

"No, ho. You're coming with." She pulls out her compact and checks her bright red lipstick in the mirror before puckering her lips.

"Me?" I ask just as Everett, whose ears perked up from across the room says, "Who?"

Peyton raises her middle finger and holds it behind her head towards Everett. "You're coming, Skyler has plans with Aidan, and can't be on Leighton duty today. She said we should go get like mani pedis or see a movie or some shit, but that's not how I keep my girl from dwelling on bullshit." She turns around and glares at Everett to drive home the part about what exactly she's referring to as 'bullshit.' "We're getting drunk."

"Pey…I appreciate the sentiment, although I don't really need a babysitter…" I glare at her.

"Clearly that was a joke, but you just found out the love of your life might have knocked up some other girl, you're allowed to be upset, you're allowed to need your friends, and you're allowed to get drunk with said friends and let hot fraternity guys get you liquored up." She glares at Everett again. "I know you've known him for like a hundred years, but people change, babe. Not everyone stays friends with their childhood friends forever."

"Enough!" Everett barks as he moves into the kitchen. I feel his anger under my skin and I know I need to calm him down before he explodes.

"Babe..." I don't know how I missed it, but the look in Peyton's eyes shows me that she's more than a few mimosas in, and she's ready to go for Everett's jugular.

"Peyton, don't start that shit." Everett's eyes are darker than their usual bright blue and I can see the tinge in his cheeks from when he's worked up.

"What shit?" She stands up and slaps her hand against the counter. "You got some other girl pregnant! When you profess to be so in love with *my* best friend!"

"She was my goddamn best friend first, Peyton. Don't talk some shit like I don't care about her or you know her better than I do."

"Okay, don't talk about me like I'm not in the room." I interrupt and stare at them both.

"Leigh, you don't need this. I know you're too close and too involved in the situation, but you're not seeing this for what it is. You're going to what? Help him raise a child with another woman he cheated on you with?"

"Peyton... stop it," I tell her. Not only did I not want to hear it, I certainly didn't want to hear it *right now* in front of Everett.

"It's bullshit." She points at me.

"Peyton, this isn't your business," Everett snarls. "And you're so desperate to not be a fifth wheel, you're using this to recruit a new wingwoman. Don't project your misery onto anyone else," he continues.

"Everett!" I shriek.

Peyton's eyes widen and she takes a step back. "You think...you think *I'm* miserable? If you do, you haven't been paying attention. What reason would I have to want to jump into a relationship? What I've seen here?" She points back and forth between me and Everett. "No, I'd rather my man not sleep with other women and get them pregnant. Nice try though. Please explain to me how *you* passed Psych. No, you're lashing out at me because I'm going to keep it real with Leighton and that scares the fuck out of you because I *might* just be able to cut through the bullshit dickmatization you have over her."

I can see Everett gearing up for his comeback so I put my hand up. "Both of you, enough," I snap and look at Everett. "Can you give us a second?" He narrows his gaze at her before he heads back up the stairs without another look at me. I glare at her before I point towards our front door. I follow her outside and close it slowly behind us. It's barely ten AM, which means it's still chilly, but it's April so it's already rounding fifty degrees.

"Listen, Leigh, I'm sorry I snapped like that." She looks contrite, and I know she does feel bad which calms me down slightly.

I'm not sure what I want to say to her. I want to yell at her and hug her and call her the worst friend and the best friend. I want to question her for judging me and thank her for vocalizing it. I'm so conflicted and I hate that the feelings of the man currently seething in my bedroom cause so much of that conflict.

"Say something," she says as she leans against the steel railing attached to our stairs.

"You think I'm dickmatized?"

Her eyes widen as if she's shocked. "You think you aren't?"

"I think Everett made a mistake, but…I do think he loves me. I know that without his dick inside of me Pey."

A door opens and Skyler steps out pulling her robe over her. "I'm getting really tired of being interrupted during sex."

"Sorry, Everett and Peyton entered World War Three." I wince.

"No, that's not what I heard. Everett knocking on my door and summoning me down here to make sure you had someone besides *the man eater's* opinion is what interrupted us. To be fair, I don't think he knew we were having sex, but still." She puts her cup of coffee to her lips and blows on the steam. "So, what's going on?"

"Everett had a fit because I want to take Leigh to a day party," Peyton says.

"It was more than that and you know it." I interject. "You made it sound like you were ready to present me to a group of horny frat brothers as a single woman." I give her a pointed glare, and Peyton shrugs.

"Look, I'm just saying you're twenty and maybe this…is a sign. God works in mysterious ways and all that."

"You aren't religious," Skyler interjects.

"I'm actually shocked you didn't just turn into a pillar of salt," I add.

Peyton smacks my shoulder and shakes her head before itching her nose ring. "Listen, are you one hundred percent sure Everett's the one? Because you better be sure before you embark on this journey with him, and I think it's going to be harder than you think getting acclimated to this new normal. Just because you've known him eleven years and you could operate his dick before you could operate a car doesn't mean he's your happily ever after. And I understand that relationships aren't easy and not everything's a walk in the park, but this might be a literal walk through hell."

I flit my eyes to Skyler who's bouncing on her heels probably because my perpetually cold friend is in hardly any clothes besides a thin silk robe. "I see her side, Leigh." Her face is sad, and I know she feels like she's letting me down. She's the optimistic one. The one in love. The happy one.

My eyes well up with tears and I scrunch my nose. "You're supposed to be Team Everett."

"I'm Team Leighton. I just…I want you to be happy. This whole thing isn't fair to you. I feel for Everett too, don't get me wrong, but whether or not he remembers," she shrugs. "He made his bed…"

"Don't feel like you have to lie in it with him." Peyton speaks up and Skyler, who I was hoping would say that wasn't where she was going with it, just nods in agreement.

"Hey." I walk into my bedroom to see Everett fully dressed and sitting on the edge of my bed with his arms resting on his knees. His head jerks up to meet mine and then he smiles like he hasn't seen me in forever. Like just me entering the room makes him feel better. But just as quick as he smiles, he frowns as if he's remembering where I've been.

"Your friends done shitting on me?"

"That's not fair, Everett."

I see the hurt all over his face and it makes my heart thump inside my chest seeing the vulnerability mar his perfect features. "It's not? So, what do you call what Peyton was saying?"

"She knows she was out of line and she apologized." I offer, weakly.

"I'm sensing a but…"

"This situation is just hard to navigate. One minute I think we can do this and the next…"

"And your friends are making it easier by judging you? Judging me?" He interrupts.

"No one is judging you, Everett."

"Peyton surely is."

"It's not judgment. She'd never judge anyone for screwing someone and accidentally getting pregnant. There's a reason she takes Plan B like it's a daily vitamin. Don't act like it's about that. She's angry at you because of *me*. And I do believe you had some choice things to say as well."

"She started it."

"I don't care who started it…"

"Leigh, I'll take shit from you but not from your friends." He snaps.

Did he seriously just say that to me? "Take shit? Really?"

"You know what I mean."

"No…not really. Enlighten me. Is that what you think this is? Taking my shit? Okay, well you can go." I shrug. *I don't want him to go, but if he wants to, so be it.*

"That's not what I meant."

"It's what you said. Literally." I snap.

"I just mean, you lashing out and being upset is I understand that, and I accept it, and I want us to work through that, but I'm not in a relationship with Peyton or Skyler." I don't say anything when he speaks up. "And I can already see they're getting to you."

"Getting to me? What the fuck? You know I'm so sick of everyone around here thinking that I have no control over my own thoughts. That I'm so heavily influenced by *your* dick or my friends. You want to hear some of my own thoughts? First off, this whole situation fucking sucks, Everett." My body starts to shake with anger and exhaustion and I know I need to rein in my temper before I lose it. "Secondly, I don't buy this bullshit *I don't remember fucking her* thing for one second. So, I'm seriously going to need you to change your narrative."

"I don't!"

I put my hand up. "I'm done with it. I love you, but…"

"No." He moves towards me. "I refuse to buy it. This can't be over." He flips my wrist over and runs his finger over the script reminding me of how deep our love really runs. "Run away with me."

"So, you're going to be a college dropout and a deadbeat dad on top of everything else?" I sniffle back a painful memory. "Kids grow up to hate those dads, remember?"

I have no memories of my birth father, and about a grand stuffed in random birthday cards in my room from being sent fifty dollars every birthday. I'd never known him, so I have never necessarily missed him. Luckily for me, I had a wonderful stepfather who filled those shoes, but it doesn't stop the gaping holes and feelings of rejection that creep in when I remember he left the second my mother learned she was pregnant.

"But *you'll* hate me." He cups my face and leans down hesitantly to brush his lips over mine. I sigh into his mouth and wrap my arms around his neck.

"Never."

"We can take it day by day. At your speed…Whatever you want. I just…I can't do this without you, Leigh."

"You don't see how selfish that is to ask this of me?" I pull away, the tears spilling out of my eyes.

"No! Because I'd do it for you! I'd do whatever it took to be with you if I knew you loved me. And I *know* you love me, Leigh."

"That's not the point! You're asking me to watch you have a baby with another woman."

"Who means nothing to me!" He interrupts, as his hands tighten around me to prevent me from moving from his grasp.

"She's going to be the mother of your child; she *should* mean something."

"I just mean…she's not you. *No one* could ever be you."

"What if your parents or her parents want you two to get married, what then?"

"You've been reading too many of your books. It's 2019. You don't have to get married just because you're having a baby." He shakes his head. "I'm not marrying anyone but you." I don't even allow myself to appreciate the fluttering in my stomach over his comment. He wants to marry me. He wants forever with me.

But what would the next nine months bring?

I'm about to respond when his phone whirls to life. He crosses the room to grab his phone and a low groan leaves his lips. "Fuck."

"Is it Alli?"

He shakes his head. "My dad. I called him when you were downstairs, and now I'm regretting everything."

"You should tell him; just get it over with."

He lets out a breath, his finger hovering over the screen. "Will you stay?"

I nod and watch as he slowly slides his finger across. "Hey, Dad." He lets out a breath. "I hope you're sitting down."

Nine

Everett

"**CARTWRIGHT!**" Coach Peck bellows from across the field.

I slow to a jog before making my way towards the sideline as my teammates continue to run laps after a shitty scrimmage that could probably be attributed to my four dropped passes. I already know Coach is going to lay into me, but I also know that despite my off day—off week, two weeks…that I'm still the best player on the team by far.

Coach Peck crosses his arms over his CGU sweatshirt and turns his hat backwards, probably so I can better see the disappointment all over his face. "I should make you run sprints till tomorrow's game," he snaps. "The hell is going on with you? You've been off your game for weeks." He glowers at me.

I can't even argue. Before this situation with Alli, I wasn't exactly giving it a hundred percent when Leighton wasn't talking to me.

I let out a breath and rub a hand over my face. "I know, Coach. But I swear, I'll be ready for tomorrow's game."

"You haven't been proving that during practice. I should bench you."

Anger slithers up my spine, his words grating over my

skin. "And put who in? Michaels? He doesn't have half the skill I do," I argue.

"At least he's focused, and I wasn't aware that I was asking for your opinion or approval. This is my goddamn team; one you've barely acted like you want to be a part of."

"Excuse me if I have a lot going on right now."

He sighs and slams his clipboard to the ground. I watch as his pen flies out and gets lost in the grass. "This is exactly why I advise my players not to start relationships going into a season…your mind is on the wrong fucking things." My eyes snap to his angry brown ones. "You think your teammates haven't ratted you out about you and the girl you've been obsessed with since the second your dick got hard for the first time?"

"It's not about her," I growl. I haven't told my teammates about Alli and thankfully she's kept it to herself as well so things haven't gotten around. But I know that it's only a matter of time. *Like when she starts showing.*

"Well, whatever it is, it's making you play like shit and I won't have you jeopardizing tomorrow's game because your head is so far up a girl's ass. You're benched."

I shake my head to keep my wayward thoughts from thinking of Leighton's ass. "Are you kidding me?"

"I'm most certainly not kidding you, and I'd advise you to watch your tone before you're benched for next week's away game too."

I swallow hard, trying to push my words down my throat before I find myself kicked off the lacrosse team completely. I was hoping to be captain next year, and I hate that in two weeks I might have killed my chances.

I sigh and swallow my pride, preparing to shed a little light into what's had me so fucked up the past few weeks. "This girl, a different girl…not my girl…is claiming she's pregnant and it's mine."

He narrows his eyes and looks behind me at my team members I know are still running laps. When his eyes turn back to me, I can sense the judgment radiating off of him. "You cheat on your girl?"

"No! Well…it's messy. The night it allegedly happened was the night Leighton and I became official." I drop to the bench with my head in my hands, grateful that my teammates and the other coaches are far enough away not to hear me. "I don't remember anything from that night."

"Even in your drunken stupor, you can't remember to wrap it up?" He scolds.

I look up to find him staring down at me like a parent scolding a child. *And God knows I've heard about enough of that the last two weeks from my parents.* "I had to have. There's no way. I had never slept with her before and for me to do it on the night I started dating Leighton, I just…"

He nods and rubs his jaw. "Listen, this blows and I get how it's affecting your concentration, but—I still have to bench you." Before I can protest, he puts a hand up. "I don't want to, and you are my best player, but your head isn't in the game."

I look out at the field to the sea of white and blue jerseys running back and forth between lines in part because of my shitty playing and let out a sigh. "Yeah. I get it."

"It's not permanent and it's not personal, Cartwright. You get that, right?"

"Yeah." I pull the practice penny off over my head and toss it to the side. "Whatever," I grumble.

Alli Chem Lab: Can we talk?

I'm still staring at the three word text as I wait for her outside of her sorority house. Sorority row is located just off campus and most importantly somewhere Leighton Mills wouldn't be caught dead. I see Alli moving down the hill towards her house, her blonde hair flowing around her and her letters stamped across her chest. "Hey, Everett." I notice her face is a little fuller and she's practically drowning in the sweatshirt over her petite frame making me wonder if she's showing and she's trying to hide it.

Are you showing at six weeks?

"Alli." I nod.

She slides her sunglasses to the top of her head revealing tired eyes. "So…how are you?"

"Been better. What's going on?" I blow off her question, not wanting to get into this now.

"What's wrong?" She furrows her brows as if she's concerned.

"Can you just tell me why you needed to meet?" I snap. I'm irritated by the day, by her, by everything, and all I want is to crawl into bed with my girl and sleep the day away.

Her eyes widen and her lips form a straight line. "Fine, excuse me for caring. Listen, my parents want to meet you."

Fuck. I let out a breath. "Like…now?"

"Yes."

"I mean is it necessary…like now?"

"Everett, I'm pregnant. They are a bit curious about the guy who contributed to that." Bile rises in my throat just like it always does when I think about what I did. *What we did.* I swallow it down and take a deep breath.

Why the hell did I not wrap it up? "I've been meaning to talk to you about it before now, but Leighton is just always…*there*."

She turns her nose up in the air and rolls her eyes in a circle.

"Alright, enough," I tell her. "The digs about Leigh are getting old. Your issue is with me, not her."

"It's about both of you. It's about the fact that I knew something was going on, and you would lie right to my face. It's about the fact that you were cheating on me...with her!"

I swallow guiltily. "I know, Alli. Trust me, I feel like shit."

"Do you? A guy that feels like shit, a guy that's even a little bit humble wouldn't berate me for not liking the girl he cheated on me with."

"I'm not berating you, but I'm not going to let you insult her either," I warn her. "Cut that shit out."

"Whatever. Will you come to brunch on Saturday or what?" Her hands fall to her hips and she cocks her head to the side.

"Brunch?" I'm fairly certain a woman in her condition shouldn't be having brunch.

She lets out an annoyed breath. "Not like a boozy brunch, obviously. Contrary to popular belief, brunch does exist without mimosas."

Said no college student, ever.

"Fine, brunch."

"Okay, so pick me up at like eleven?"

"Pick you up? Alli, it's not a date. I'll meet you at the restaurant." I don't even wait for her to protest before I'm walking away from her and back up the hill towards campus. "Text me where," I call over my shoulder.

I slam my front door closed, grateful that I don't see Pat or Dave in their usual spots on the couch and toss my backpack to the floor in front of the door. I'm so over this shit. I feel like my head is spinning between practice and Alli. It feels as if my entire life is going up in flames and to top it off, my relationship with Leighton is so fragile, I'm scared to breathe. I trudge up the stairs, prepared to take the longest nap, knowing that Leighton is still in class when a familiar perfume surrounds me. I push my door open to see Leighton sitting on my bed, cross legged and staring at the door like she's waiting for me to come in.

"Well, this is a nice surprise." I smile at her as my legs eat the distance between us and press a kiss to her lips. "I thought you had class?"

"Canceled," she whispers, "and I wanted to be here." I'd sent her a text after practice letting her know that I had been benched and after a string of sad face emojis she told me she'd see me later and she'd make it all better. I sit on the bed next to her and she immediately climbs into my lap before wrapping her arms around my neck. "I'm sorry." She peppers kisses down my cheek and neck and I grab her jaw to look at her.

"You have nothing to be sorry for." I press a kiss to her forehead and hold her tighter to my body. "I'm so glad you're here." I pull her hair from her high ponytail and submerge my face in it, letting the smell of her tresses calm me. "This day has just been so shitty."

"Why? What else?"

I take a deep breath as I prepare myself for a potential argument. "Alli wants me to meet her parents."

She tenses in my arms and just as I rub my hand down her bare arm to calm her, I feel her pulling away and out of my arms. I try to hold onto her, but she's out of my grip and sitting next to me. "Why?" She scrunches her face together and wraps her arms around herself.

"Leighton..."

"Why do you need to meet her parents? Is she introducing you as her boyfriend?"

"No! No way. She knows I'm with you."

"Really? Because this whole 'meet the parents' thing doesn't sound like she knows that."

"Her parents want to meet me. What am I supposed to say? No?" *Trust me, I wanted to. The last thing I want is to meet Alli's parents. Talking to any girl's parents in this situation is scary as fuck, but talking to a girl's parents I have no plans to be with? Makes me sound like an asshole and I'm not looking forward to being that person.*

Leighton lets out a sigh and stares at the door, and I wonder if she's preparing herself to leave. "Just brunch?"

"What do you mean?"

"Are you like...spending the day together like some big happy fucking family?" She stands up and crosses her arms and I take note of her toned legs that I regret won't be wrapped around my waist anytime soon.

"Baby...it's not like that."

She squeezes her eyes shut and shakes her head. "But it *is* like that. You and...*her* and this baby. You're a family. A family I'm not a part of."

I'm off the bed instantly cupping her face in my hand. "*You're* my family."

She pulls out of my grasp, a sad smile finding her lips that shatters me. I can almost hear the words swirling around her brain. The *"well, actually..."* The thought that even though she knows she's a huge part of my life, that this is part of my life I accidentally excluded her from. That she's only family by proxy. That Alli will have a difficult time accepting *her* as family. And while Leighton doesn't give a shit, eventually she'll give up the fight because Alli is the mother and Leighton *is not*.

"Sure, Everett," she sighs, defeatedly.

I pull into the parking lot attached to Sorority Row and let out a sigh as the anxiety unfurls in my chest. The throbbing that started at my temples has somehow moved to my chest, making it tight and almost impossible to breathe easily. Despite my protests, I'm now picking Alli up because one of her sorority sisters "needed her car *super* last minute." As much as I want to tell her to take an Uber, begrudgingly I told her yes when she begged me to pick her up. I take a deep breath, trying to alleviate the pressure when my phone chirps with an alert. Part of me is afraid to open it, knowing that people are day drinking at Leighton's. She told me to come over after, and quite frankly, I can't wait until I can use alcohol and a drunk Leighton to erase what I predict will be a difficult day.

I make my way out of my car, wishing I could take a shot to calm my nerves when Alli comes out of the house. She's wearing a navy sundress and flats underneath a white sweater, with a sun hat on her head making me wonder if this is all a ploy and we're actually doing that cliché fraternity-sorority trip to *Foxfields*. An occasion that has all of Greek life looking like Ralph Lauren models, pretending to watch horses race in between chugging *Veuve Clicquot* champagne straight from the bottle.

On the outside, Alli is a polished debutante that has been groomed for this all her life, making her a legacy at CGU and inevitable president of her sorority when the time comes. She waves at me, and as soon as I'm within arm's reach she pushes herself into my arms. "Thank you for doing this." She squeezes a beat too long and when I try to pull away, I notice the look in her eye. *Hope.*

Well, fuck. What is she thanking me for, exactly? As much as I don't want to go through the awkward formalities of meeting the parents of the girl I accidentally got pregnant, I know it needs to be done. "Ummm, yeah…sure."

"You'll have to let me know when yours are in town." I freeze, thinking about how that would go down. Especially since I'd want Leighton there.

Not to mention my parents are angry and disappointed. I don't think I've seen the full extent of their fury and won't until a paternity test is complete. Evidently, they're as skeptical as the rest of us. Particularly my dad but probably because he's a lawyer and rarely believes anything without proof, especially once he gets the full uncensored story about Alli's and my relationship and Leighton's involvement with the demise of it.

I don't respond because the idea of her meeting my parents is another formality I don't want to think about. "Do you want to come in? I'm almost finished getting ready."

I think about just saying I'll wait outside but I figure that having a bad attitude isn't the way to get out of this alive, so I agree and make my way inside behind her. "Do you want to come up?" she asks as she stands at the bottom of her stairs, that look of hope still in her eyes and my eyes flash to hers angrily.

"No, Alli. I don't, and I've been clear about why. I want to be cordial, but don't mistake that for anything else. We are *not* together, and I suggest you not try and pretend we are because I'm not going to play along." My posture is rigid, my fists clenching at my sides, not because I want to hurt her or anyone, but because I'm frustrated. And angry that Leighton had predicted this. She's been nervous over the fact that Alli may try to use this as a way to get me to choose her, and that she'd try and put on a show for her parents.

She blinks her eyes several times, and I note the glistening in her eyes. "Can you at least pretend that you *like* me? I didn't do this to make *your* life hard, Everett. We are both in this situation and turning on me isn't helping."

"Neither is flirting with me or whatever it is you're doing."

"I wasn't flirting. I asked if you wanted to come upstairs because my sisters are in the kitchen drinking and I didn't want them to bother you because news flash: they're not your biggest fans." She scoffs. "But fine, wait here."

I run a hand through my hair. *Fuck. Get a grip, Everett.* I need to stop acting like all of this is an act brought on by a woman scorned.

Even if she is.

Ten

Leighton

We're rounding hour three of shots and beer bongs and mimosas and Everett has essentially gone ghost. I'd texted and Snapchatted and even tried to FaceTime him, all which have gone unanswered. I know he's with Alli's parents, but exacerbated by all of the shots and beers and mimosas, I've grown irate at the fact that I'm being ignored to appease them. *Irate and slightly irrational.*

Okay, completely irrational.

There are moments of clarity I have while drunk. Moments where I already know I'm going to regret my drunk behavior in the morning. The moment where I say a silent apology to my sober self that I'll have to deal with the aftermath of acting like a complete asshole. Or in this case, the psycho girlfriend that guys so eloquently call us.

That moment comes after the second text.

And then again after the third call.

I'm drunk.

And angry.

And hurt.

And drunk.

And I have more than enough self-awareness to know that

it's a dangerous combination.

"Why..." I sniffle as I sit on the edge of my bathtub. "Why aren't you here? Or taking my calls?" The tears slide down my cheeks as the devastation I'm trying to keep locked away seeps through my brain and pours from my mouth. "How long does brunch have to be? It's been three hours and...can you just come be with me?" I sniffle again. "I hate this so much. I hate that I've been reduced to...this. An...afterthought. I miss being important. Even before we were together, I knew I was important, and now...now you won't even take my calls." My lip trembles just as fast footsteps move up the stairs and into my bedroom and then my two best friends are standing in front of me, holding cups full of liquor looking at me with sad and angry eyes.

Skyler holds her hand out as Peyton speaks. "Give us the phone, *now.*"

"Call me." My voice shakes as I press the end button and squeeze my eyes together.

"You're better than this, Leigh," Skyler says.

"Better than my pain? I don't think that's possible." A flair of jealousy ripples through me as I think about Skyler with her perfect relationship and Peyton with her contentedness over being single. They're both happy with their uncomplicated relationship status while I spend so much time feeling nauseous and jealous and anxious and sad and *betrayed.*

There's that word I try not to think about because it *is* a mistake. And he *doesn't* remember. And we *weren't* together. There are so many complications and gray areas that make me feel like I shouldn't feel betrayed because he'd never betray me.

But it doesn't stop the way I feel because feelings are beyond reason and rationale, which I barely have any of in the first place after three shots of tequila.

"Give me your phone." Peyton takes a long sip from her straw and narrows her gaze before tucking a sleek blonde strand behind her ear.

"No, I'm fine. No more calls." I try to protest.

"Yeah, bullshit," Peyton argues. "You're going to hate yourself tomorrow."

I swallow, hearing what I already know spoken aloud. "Why isn't he answering?"

"Because he's at some Stepford family brunch and he's got manners!" Peyton says and I can hear the exasperation in her voice. "Maybe Alli took his phone. Maybe they took him into some dungeon in Virginia with no service and have him tied up in the corner where they plan to keep him until Alli gives birth. Take your pick." Peyton shrugs.

"Pey! You're not helping." Skyler puts her hand up and sits next to me on the tub, putting her hand over mine. "Everett adores you. He's probably sitting at the table, thinking about you, but he doesn't want to be on his phone the whole time. It's like sitting in a class where you know the teacher is a stickler about texting. Now imagine the attention is completely on you. He's probably being grilled and questioned and that means he can't entertain all of your drunk texts and calls," she says, and even in my drunken stupor I can tell she's placating me slightly.

"But what if I needed him?" *He's never not...been there.*

"Babe, he was answering here and there at first, but you're drunk and he knows that, and he knows that I'm here and Peyton is here and Pat and Dave are here."

"But *he's* not here." I pout.

"And is calling him nonstop going to change that?" Sincerity radiates from her brown eyes like an older sister I never had, despite being six months younger than me.

"Phone." Peyton presses and finally I acquiesce, placing my phone in her hand.

"Tell me if he calls or texts or…"

"Yes, yes whatever." She slides it into her back pocket of her jeans. "Now come on, let's go whip the guys at flip cup."

A few rounds of flip cup, and only one text from Everett that told me he loved me and would see me soon, and I'm officially over it. We were rounding five o'clock making me wonder what the fuck kind of brunch went five hours unless he somehow got hammered with her parents.

Most people have left to go home to shower for the night or nap or eat, leaving me, Peyton, and Skyler alone with Everett's roommates.

"This sucks so much." I hiccup before taking a swig of champagne straight from the bottle. The bubbles settle on top of all the alcohol I've drunk and I can feel myself nearing the end of my rope.

"Maybe you should have some water," Pat says.

"Or maybe," Dave enters the living room wielding his bong, "this will clear your mind. Mellow you out some." He lights the top and takes a hit before passing it to me.

"I AM mellow!"

"No, you're not. You're high strung as fuck," Dave adds.

"Do you blame me?" I shriek.

"Can you not poke the bear?" Peyton says as she snatches the bong away from Dave. "And don't give her that, she's too hammered and it'll put her way the fuck in her feelings. Have you never smoked with a girl before? Goddamn rookie." She rolls her eyes and takes a hit before handing it to Pat.

"We can't blame you, but E has a lot on his plate, and you being crazy isn't helping," Pat says and Peyton and Skyler shoot him a look.

"Do you know *anything* about women?" Skyler narrows her eyes angrily and puts her hands on her hips.

Pat's eyes shift between all three of us but give me a sad look. "I didn't…sorry." He shakes his head.

"He doesn't know shit," Dave adds. "He just means, him thinking you're mad at him or you're going to leave him when he *does* need you, isn't helping."

I lean back on my couch, putting my feet up on the coffee table in front of me and let my head fall back against the cushions. "I just miss when it was easy. When we didn't have this big uncomfortable elephant lurking in the corner."

"Is Alli the elephant? Because she's pregnant?" Pat asks, his dilated eyes blinking in rapid succession.

"Wow, are you stoned." Skyler snorts before shaking her head. She looks down at her lap and then suddenly she hops up. "Oh! Aidan's calling." She cheers before running out of the room.

"See, why can't I have that?" I pout as I point after her.

"Because *your* boyfriend's a dumbass and Aidan's got like twelve degrees thereby *not* a dumbass," Peyton interjects as she waves her hand.

"That's not fair. We don't even know if the baby's his!" Dave argues.

"I'm still not convinced," Pat says as he slides his hat to the back and cracks another beer. He takes a sip before continuing. "He's crazy about you, Leigh. Seriously, insane. I just can't see him fucking Alli."

I cringe hearing the words spelled out so crassly. "Can you not?"

"Sorry, *making love* to Alli," Pat corrects himself

"That's worse!" I punch his shoulder before getting up

and bounding up the stairs to my bedroom. I drop to my bed, the weight of Pat's words weighing on my heart making me want to lie down and just *forget*.

A hand rubbing my back pulls me out my sleep, and I feel groggy and disoriented, and for a moment, I wonder if I'm still drunk or crossing into hangover territory.

"Baby." I hear the word in my ear, his breath dancing down my neck and instantly, I'm wet.

My eyes flutter open and I note it's still light out, though I'm not sure what time it is exactly. When I turn in his arms, I find sad, worried eyes. He pulls me closer to him and presses a kiss to my forehead.

"You ignored me," I tell him as my bottom lip pops out.

Definitely still drunk.

"I didn't mean to…" He trails off. "I just…it was hard to keep responding to you amidst them rapid fire asking me questions. I was in the hot seat for hours."

"About what?"

"Everything." He shakes his head before turning on his back. "Can we just not talk about it? I just want to lie with you and forget about everything but you and me."

"It's not that easy," I tell him as I sit up and feel the bubbles from the champagne swirling around my brain. "And maybe now it's *easier* to ignore what's happening, but eventually there will be a baby you'll be in charge of, and it'll be harder to ignore a world outside of you and me."

"Leighton—" He starts when his phone chirps from the nightstand on what has become *his side* of the bed. He ignores the first chime until it begins to ring. "God, WHAT?" he barks as he reaches for his phone. "Dave, what do you want? I'm with—wait, what? No, hold on." He pulls his phone away from his ear and taps his screen a few times and his eyes immediately widen. "Son of a fucking bitch," he growls, and I frown and try and lean over to see, but he taps out of it and puts his phone back to his ear. "Thanks for calling me, that's bullshit, you know. Yeah…well, thanks."

"What's wrong?" I cock my head to the side, wondering what could have caused him to get so agitated with his best friend when he lets out a sigh.

"Alli…posted something. I guess at brunch. I didn't even realize it." He hands me his phone and I click on the Instagram story which shows her smiling for the camera and him looking down at his phone with the words *"when bae won't pay attention."* I frown and tap the screen to see a picture with only her and her parents that I'm assuming Everett took for them. I tap again. Pretentious pictures of their food. *Tap.* And then finally a video showing that the four of them were at brunch. Though *again,* it doesn't seem like Everett's even paying attention in the split second she showed him. "Say something."

"She's sending a message…to me, I'm sure." I toss the phone down the bed and shake my head.

"I am so fucking pissed," he growls and gets off the bed to pace back and forth. "I'm calling her."

"To say what?"

"Well first, to take it the fuck down. I made it clear we weren't together and her parents don't think anything differently. This wasn't some pretend *Meet the Parents* bullshit. I made it clear that this was an accident and we weren't going to be together just because we're in this situation."

"And? What does that matter? Quite frankly her parents' opinions are irrelevant. She's making a fool out of me *and* you." I wrap my arms around my body and speak the words that I don't want but I *need*. "I think you should go."

"Go? Wait…Leigh."

"I can barely handle *this*; I don't know what I'm going to do when she starts showing or tells people she's pregnant. She's not going to make this easy. She posted that so there won't be any question of paternity when people learn she's pregnant."

"I sure as fuck can question it and *will*. She knows I'm requesting a paternity test. But aside from that, she can't *make* me be with her."

"No, but she can make it really hard for you to be with *me*."

His eyebrows shoot to his hairline. "How? I…I would do anything to be with you."

The words gut me because I would do anything as well, but it seems like breaking my own heart over and over again is what is required to be with him. I want better for myself. *I deserve better.* "I know." I let out a sigh, grateful that I wasn't more drunk when I saw her Instagram story for the first time because I probably would have broken something. "I'm drunk and tired and I really do think you should go."

His cheeks turn red and he furrows his brow. "Leigh, are you breaking up with me?"

My lips form a straight line as I look towards my window and watch as the sun sets over D.C. creating an eerie, sad glow in my bedroom. "I don't know."

"Leighton, please…I love you." His voice shakes and I can already hear the emotion building.

"I know you do." I look up at him, and I can feel the tears forming in my throat and the back of my eyes. The tingle shoots through my chest and face, like when I'm about to break down in sobs. "But I just know myself."

"I can't lose you," he whispers and when I don't say

anything, he drops to his knees in front of me. *"Please,"* he begs. *"Don't do this. Don't break us."*

And just that quickly, I've gone from sad to *furious*. "ME?!" I shoot up to my feet so fast his eyes widen and he's knocked slightly off balance. "I BROKE US?" I scream. I scream so loud I know Skyler and Peyton are probably already pouring the shots for when this is over. "YOU," I point my finger at him, "YOU *fucked* some bitch the NIGHT we decided to be together." He starts to speak and I put my hand up. "I AM TALKING," I growl. "You fucked her, and I *forgave* you. We moved on. We were happy. I chalked it up to you being drunk and confused and maybe Alli manipulated you with some shit about being hurt that you'd cheated on her with me. I don't know." I put my hands over my eyes as I speak the ludicrousness out loud.

I made excuses for him.

I rationalized his mistake.

I let him back in when I should have closed the door on us forever because I thought that maybe he really hadn't slept with her.

How could I have been so stupid?

"And THEN, she comes back and tells us she's *pregnant!* And she's vindictive and manipulative and wants you and HATES ME. She's *always* hated me. You used some girl to make me jealous because you didn't have the balls to tell me you had feelings for me. AND LOOK WHERE THAT GOT US! Now this girl somehow has feelings for you AND your baby inside her! And you have the audacity to say *I* broke us?" My chest is heaving, my eyes are wide and my throat is sore from quite literally screaming. "How dare you?"

"Leigh, I know, I fucked up and—"

"I never want to speak to you again," I snap. *You don't*

mean that, my subconscious screams. *Tell him you don't mean that!*

"Wh—what? No, Leigh, you don't mean that." He says, his eyes wide and full of worry. When I don't immediately answer, he takes my hands in his and rubs his lips over them. "I need you." He says quietly.

"No, you don't. You need to take responsibility and be there for Alli and your baby. There's no room for me anymore, at least not right now."

"Of course, there is. You'll always be the most important person to me, and you know that." He stands to his feet and I take a step back putting my hands up.

"I just can't watch you do this with another woman. A woman that doesn't respect me or us and—"

He runs a hand through his hair and for a moment I'm transported back to when we were much younger. The younger Leighton and Everett would probably be horrified at us both. "So, you don't love me enough to stick it out with me?"

My heart hurts hearing him phrase it like that. Like it's as simple as loving him or not loving him. He hurt me, broke my heart, and unless I let him go now, he's just going to continue to do so. Even if it's inadvertently. Every time he goes to a doctor's appointment with her, or sees her, instead of spending time with me, the irrational side of me will lose its fucking mind. And that's *before* the baby is even born.

What happens when it's born and becomes the center of his universe?

What happens when Alli gives birth and he starts to see her as the mother of the baby that he loves and adores and not just the girl he got pregnant?

"I guess I don't." I put a hand over my chest to try and

ease the pain of my heart breaking inside of it.

"You don't mean that," he says immediately.

"It doesn't matter what I mean or not. You know how I feel about you, Everett, but...at some point, I have to choose what's right for me. And this? It's not right for me." I twist my mouth to stop myself from crying. "I'm sorry. I just...I can't."

"So, I can't even keep you as my best friend?" His face is pained, worse than the time they lost the lacrosse championship in high school. Worse than the night his dad moved out. Worse than the night we were stupid teenagers and got alcohol citations when the cops busted our friend's party. "I can't have you at all?" he asks.

"Can...can I just have some space?"

He lets out a breath, dropping his head in defeat and rubs the space under his eyes. "Space from me? No talking...at all?" He twists his mouth and even from this angle I know he's gritting his teeth.

The tears have formed, and are sliding down my cheeks fast, but I don't make a move to wipe them away and neither does he and I briefly wonder if he's afraid to touch me. "I don't know. For now, yes."

He looks up at me and his blue eyes are glistening that beautiful shade of blue that only comes out the few times he's really worked up. It's a shame this is the only time I can see it because it is a truly beautiful color. "But...I love you. I only want you," he begs.

"I know." I nod because I don't doubt Everett's love for me. It isn't about that. It's about so many other factors, and all of them lead up to the fact that we're only twenty and dealing with real life things that I'm not ready for. I'm not ready to be a stepmom or be with a man that already had, for lack of a better phrase, *baby mama drama*. I want to be free to travel after college and make mistakes and not worry about screwing up a child. And then, of course, there's the niggling thought in the back of my head that says that maybe I've been in the way of Alli and Everett being together long term. Maybe they're the endgame, and *I* have been just a bump in the road. I'm the security blanket that he eventually needed to be free from. She's pregnant and having a baby, *their* baby, and that does mean something.

Potentially more than eleven years of friendship.

Eleven

Everett

GOD, I MISS HER. IT'S BEEN A FULL WEEK SINCE I'VE TALKED to Leighton. Seven full days and it's the longest we've ever gone without speaking. Well, it's the longest she's gone without speaking to me. I've texted her and called her and left her voicemails. Sent her emails to her school email and her personal Gmail. I've left messages with Skyler and Peyton and sent her flowers and pizza and *Georgetown Cupcake* that I'm pretty sure her roommates ate before she even saw them. I sent her balloons because even though they don't necessarily say *I'm sorry*, she loves them and they make her happy, and I've been praying that it would make her smile, if only for a moment.

A smile, I would have caused.

I'm sitting on my couch, holding a bottle of whiskey under my arm when Pat comes in.

"You been here all day?" It's a Saturday, and I have no plans to leave this couch in the immediate future. I managed to go to all my classes and practice and go through the motions of my life, all while feeling the absence of Leigh on my heart and in my mind and in my soul. I feel her like a phantom limb every time I move, so deeply that my body physically aches for her.

"Yep," I tell him as I unscrew the cap and take another long swig.

"You want to go out?" I shoot him a look and raise an eyebrow at him before turning the channel to SportsCenter. "Want me to see if the girls are going out?"

"I doubt it. It's been social media silence from the three of them all week and it's driving me crazy. Skyler posted her freaking Starbucks latte yesterday and I about fell off my chair when my phone chirped with the alert."

"You have all three of them set up with alerts?" He shoots me an incredulous look.

"Sure do." I put up a hand. "Save it. I want to see her, and if the only way I can is through their eyes, then so be it."

"Why not just show up at her house?" He shrugs.

"She asked for space."

"So?"

"So, I should respect that. She doesn't want me to fight for her. Not now. She doesn't know what she wants."

"She wants you, E. Anyone can see that."

"Maybe not with all my fucking baggage." I sigh.

He doesn't say anything before kicking his shoes off and pulling out his phone. "You want pizza?"

Leighton

I'm lying on the couch, staring at the television as I round hour seven of FRIENDS. Or maybe hour eight? I pull the blanket up around my neck and take a deep breath, trying to will the pain, the nausea, the sadness away. I try to turn my brain off to focus on my favorite show when the door swings open and Skyler walks in. Peyton is on the adjacent loveseat, watching alongside, though I think she's fallen asleep. When Skyler turns on the light and I wince at the burst of illumination just as Peyton whines.

"Why are you guys sitting in the pitch black?"

"It's not. I have a candle lit." I point at our only source of light other than the TV that smells like April rain and spring and happier times.

"Turn it off, I was napping!" Peyton demands.

"It's six-thirty. Peyton, don't you think we should go out?"

"Ugh, Leighton and I decided to have a lazy weekend." She says as she snuggles further into her blanket.

"Exactly," I say from my place on the couch. "Go hang with Aidan."

"Oh, what? I'm not invited? That's bullshit." She plops on the sofa next to me and pulls her jacket off. "I just came from hanging out with Aidan. I figured we'd do something tonight."

"Well, this is what I plan on doing," I say as I point at the television.

"Everett leave any more gifts today?" She looks at Peyton and then around the room to see if he'd sent anything else. I have at least three dozen assorted flowers around the room that I don't have the heart to throw away…but I also don't have the stomach to keep them in my room either. All his gifts do is remind me that we aren't speaking. That he's left a huge hole in my chest that I've spent a week trying to fill.

Speaking of which.

"Are there any more cupcakes?" I look up and Skyler and Peyton share a look. "Did you guys eat the rest?"

"I'll order you more!" Skyler says, opening up her phone and frantically pressing some buttons, probably because she assumes I'm pissed that she and Peyton tore into my treats that Everett sent.

"Don't bring that shit in here. I had to work out another hour every day this week thanks to those little fuckers."

"Well, no one told you to eat four."

"They're crack!" Peyton looks at Skyler before falling back on the couch. "Order some more red velvets."

"He did text me again." I tell them.

"What did it say?" Skyler asks.

"Thinking about you." I close my eyes, staring at the ceiling as a tear slides down my temple and into my hair. I snort and shake my head "Funny, because I can't stop thinking about him."

"Leigh…" Skyler grabs my leg and rubs it under my blanket. "I'm going to go change, and then we can order some food?"

Skyler heads out of the room and I look over at Peyton. "Am I being a bitch for not responding?" My lips form a straight line as I realize what I asked and more importantly *who* I asked. "Right. Know my audience."

She flips me off before sitting up. "You're not being a bitch; you did ask for space. But I also know you do love him, so I don't think responding would hurt. Maybe you could just say 'same.'" She shrugs. "But I know you're worried about getting sucked back in. I know you can get wrapped up in the whirlwind, but you're in control of this situation, Leigh. Only you can decide what's right for you. When you talk, if you decide to meet up, if you take him back. But, I will say, all of this back and forth isn't healthy. If you take him back again, you need to say the past is in the past and take everything that comes in stride. Accept his faults and his mistakes and forgive. Maybe it'll be hard to forget, or even impossible, but you have to forgive. You can't punish him forever."

I'm shocked at Peyton's insight and she rolls her eyes at my shock that I know is written all over my face. "Don't look at me like that. I do take *some* things seriously. Just because I don't have any interest in being in a relationship doesn't mean I wouldn't know how to be in one."

After a weekend of vegging out on my couch with my two best friends, I don't feel anything except a few pounds heavier in my stomach and in my heart. I'm walking through campus, my earbuds jammed in my ears, as the sounds of Britney Spears *Toxic* blare through them. I close my eyes and it's almost like I'm back at my senior prom dancing with Everett in that gorgeous ballroom in the hotel in downtown Phoenix. We'd decided to go together our senior year when neither of us wanted to take a date. We spent the night dancing and laughing and sweating and then fucking in a hotel that we'd convinced our parents it would be *much easier* to stay at instead of coming home after the after party. *A party that we'd ditched anyway.*

How had I not noticed then that he loved me? Looking back, the signs were all there. The way he touched me and looked at me and cared for me. His love for me was so obvious that I feel stupid for not noticing it sooner. If I had, we would have avoided this whole situation. There'd be no Alli, no baby, no breakup. I pull my bag up higher on my shoulder and my eyes scan the South quad for Peyton or Skyler. I'm supposed to meet them for lunch, but I don't see them anywhere. I sit at a table by myself, setting my stuff next to me and letting my head fall in my hands as my elbows rest on the table. A cool April breeze whips through the air and I feel a chill shoot through me. I pull my coat tighter around me, grateful that I'd brought it despite the promise of sixty-degree weather today. *God D.C. weather is fickle. I miss Arizona. Everything about Arizona.*

I look around the quad again looking for either of my friends when I spot *him* at a table far away, staring straight at me. I turn away from him, the tears springing to my eyes and not being prepared to see him. Especially now. Makeup-less, my hair pulled into a messy, dirty bun, and a sweatshirt under my coat that I may have slept in last night.

Not that Everett cares. Every time Everett's ever told me how beautiful I am, how perfect I am, how he's never seen anything so beautiful comes flying into my brain like a montage and my heart flutters. I turn my head back towards the table and frown when I don't see him there anymore. I turn over my other shoulder, looking for him and for a moment I wonder if maybe he wasn't ever there. Perhaps I'd imagined him and my mind was just playing tricks on me.

"Looking for me? Sorry, I'm so late. I had to stay after and talk to my professor." Peyton pushes her sunglasses to her head and sits down across from me, pulling out her Smartwater and a burger from the dining hall. "Shit, it's cold out here though. Wanna eat inside?"

Everett

Fuck, she looked pretty, I think as I head off the South quad. It had taken everything in me not to go over and talk to her, but when she turned away from me, I took it as a sign that she definitely didn't want to talk.

Is she done with me for good?

I saw her shiver when the wind blew, and I wanted nothing more than to warm her up in my arms. I'm heading towards my car when my phone rings. I let my head fall back when I see who's calling and reluctantly answer. These days I screen her and let her text me if it's really important, after the last two calls were just *calling to say hey* and *do you want to grab dinner and talk?*

"Hey, Alli."

"Hey, Everett. Listen, I have a doctor's appointment next week, I was wondering if you'd be able to go with me?"

"Yeah, I…I think that's a good idea." I close my eyes and hear my dad's words in my ear. He was skeptical but until I have proof that the child isn't mine, I need to step up.

"Great, thank you," she says and then she's silent.

"Was there something else?" I ask her, already regretting asking because I know it's going to be something that involves meeting up now.

"Well…yeah, I just…I was wondering if you were busy right now?"

"Yes," I tell her, "I have to study."

"Well, we could study together or…"

"No, I'm heading home, and I just want to be by myself."

"Oh…I mean, you can just say you're hanging out with Leighton. You don't have to lie." She chuckles nervously.

"Leighton and I are taking some time apart." As soon as I say it, I don't know why I told her that. Maybe because I want her to know the chaos she's brought to my life. *Or that we both brought to my life.* Maybe a part of me feels like she should feel bad, or that I want her to feel guilty.

I know I need to stop thinking that this is her fault when it isn't. But in the deep dark crevices of my mind, I do feel like that. I blame her, myself, and everyone for this shitty situation that has taken over my life and cost me Leighton as well as my goddamn sanity.

"Oh. I didn't know."

"Well, now you do."

"Do you want to talk about it?"

"No, I don't. And you don't want to hear about it, so I don't know why you're asking. You just want to stick your nose where it doesn't belong. Or I don't know relish in the fact that Leighton is hurting and you hate her."

"You make me sound like a monster, Everett. I'm not that mean." My lips form a straight line as I think about the fact that she's right. She isn't mean, *per se*. She hates Leighton because she's the girl I cheated on her with. Alli hates her because, even before she learned of my infidelity, she knew that Leighton was the most important woman in my life by a landslide.

So, I guess her hate is warranted.

"Sorry, I don't think you're a monster. I'm just not in the mood to talk."

"Okay." She relents. "Well, if you change your mind, let me know."

"Fine…" I swallow and look to the sky, praying for patience or peace or tolerance or whatever a higher power could grant me to get me off the phone now. "Thank you."

"Talk to you later," she says and she hangs up before I can say another word.

Now, you listen to my prayers.

Twelve

Leighton

One Month Later

"I can't believe you're letting me drag you out tonight!" Peyton cheers as she bounces up and down, her blonde waves blowing in the slight wind. We are walking down Main Street towards this bar that's offering two for one shots from nine to eleven in honor of the last week of classes. Finals don't start until next week, so I'm allowing myself one night to cut loose before I hole up in the library for the better part of next week. Not that I really need to. The one benefit of breaking up with Everett and also my own heart, is I've been studying my ass off. I don't do much but eat, sleep, and study. I started conditioning for the upcoming fall season for soccer last week, but other than that I don't do much else. This is the first time I've been out in weeks and I'll admit it feels good. "Sky is so jealous."

"Somehow I doubt that." I tuck a curled hair behind my ear. "Skyler is holed up at some bed and breakfast in Virginia with her hot boyfriend, getting the shit fucked out of her. Somehow, I don't think she cares that we're going out." I roll my eyes and smooth down my dress. It's hotter than hell even at nine-thirty, and I'm glad I decided against bringing a jacket. My back is out, my legs are out, and though my tits are covered, Peyton told me I look thoroughly fuckable. Normally, I would send a picture to Everett, but I settled for posting something on my Instagram story that shows I'm going out, and more importantly *what* I'm wearing.

He was the first to view it.

I stared at my phone for a full minute after, waiting for him to respond to it, and I'll admit my heart sank when I realized he wasn't going to say anything.

Because I told him I need space and I haven't said otherwise since the night he left my house. I don't respond to any of his texts or calls and now in the past week they've stopped altogether.

We make it to the bar and flash our fakes at the bouncer who waves us in without another thought. There are people surrounding the bar, smoking and talking, and I scan the outdoor perimeter, briefly wondering if I'd see Everett. I know I asked for space but after two shots of tequila after a month of sobriety inspired by heartbreak, I realize I want anything but.

"Pey."

She doesn't look at me as she scans the bar. "Yeah, babe?"

The tequila fueled words are flying out of my mouth before I can stop them. "I want to call Everett."

Her eyes snap to mine and flicker. "Fuck, I knew the second shot was a mistake. No, we talked about this," she scolds.

"I know. I know I said I didn't want to call him." I shake my head, my heart slowly starting to pound at the idea of seeing him. *Shit, not drinking for a month has turned me into a lightweight.* "But I still love him so much, and I—" I stop talking when I sense eyes on me. Deep blue eyes that I know better than anyone are currently undressing me from across the room.

"Oh God dammit, Leigh, let's go." I feel her hand around my bicep tugging me towards the door, but I don't move.

"No…I…" I stutter as I feel my skin heat under his gaze. I watch as he downs his drink in one gulp and passes his friends to make his way over to me. Peyton is still pulling on my arm, trying to get me to follow her, but my feet are rooted to the spot, as if they're nailed there. I bite my bottom lip that's painted red and stare up at him as he approaches me.

The love of my freaking life.

The one who got away.

The one I pushed away.

"Hi, beautiful." He smiles and my eyes widen at his comment. *He still…wants me? After all those horrible things I said? After telling him I never wanted to talk to him again?* "I know you said you wanted space but—"

I don't let him continue before I'm in his arms, squeezing him *hard*. I wrap my arms around his neck and push my face harder into his black t-shirt. His arms immediately go around my back to stroke the bare skin and then I feel his lips on my temple. "I'm sorry," he whispers. "I just had to come over because you're so fucking beautiful and…"

I rub under my eyes and shake my head before pulling back. "I've missed you."

His eyebrows shoot to his hairline and a sad smile finds his face. "You have no fucking idea." We stare at each other for a second, like we're just seeing each other for the first time.

I break the silence. "I went to your game last weekend…" I whisper.

"You did?"

"I did, you played well." I nod. I went because I was trying to be supportive of my best friend. I know lacrosse is important to him and despite not speaking, I wanted to be there. And also, I longed to see him. I sat in the stands, wearing one of his jerseys underneath my jacket huddled with Skyler under an umbrella as a warm spring rain trickled down around us.

"I'd let everything slip through my fingers. You, lacrosse, my friends...even Pat and Dave got sick of my moping. The only thing that hasn't suffered are my grades, though I did bomb a biochem exam. Finally, my dad and brother flew out and told me to get my ass together if I wanted a shot at getting you back."

"Me?" *His father and brother said that? They want him with me? Not with Alli?*

"I was walking around feeling sorry for myself, and hating the world... and I relied too much on you to make me feel better. I relied too much on you to be my salvation in this shitty situation. But...I wasn't being yours."

My lip trembles and I turn my gaze to the left expecting to see Peyton, but she's disappeared into the crowd of drunk students who are shaking their asses to Rihanna. I turn back to Everett and look him over. His biceps peek out of his black t-shirt and his jeans hug him in all the right places making the space between my legs thump with need. I miss him. I miss him *there*. "Want to get a drink?" He nods towards the bar. I start to follow him but then hesitate.

"I should stay here, so Peyton doesn't think I disappeared." I point at the floor indicating, where I'd wait.

"I'll get it for you. Vodka soda?" His lips quirk up in a half smile and the dull throb between my legs turns more aggressive.

"Yes, please." I nod and it worries me that something so minute as knowing my drink order makes my heart flutter and I can sense my guard flying down with ease.

It's why I'd asked for space. *Demanded* it. Everett knows

how to suck me back in. He knows how to make me love him. He's been doing it since the fourth grade. I'm staring after him with an almost dreamlike expression when a nightmare takes form.

"What do you think you're doing?" I turn my head to see two girls that look like literal clones of Alli sizing me up and down. They're both dressed in almost identical miniskirts and matching tops and I fight the urge to call them Thing One and Thing Two. "Our *friend* is pregnant with his baby. He doesn't want you."

I narrow my gaze. My knee jerk reaction is to snap, to argue, to yell. But I realize this is probably only to get a rise out of me. I attempt to take the high road, with a flick of my hair over my shoulder. "You don't even believe that."

"Oh really? Then why are he and Alli trying to work it out?" Blonde number one says. She takes a dramatic sip of her drink and blinks her eyes at me several times.

"Okay, and if you expect me to believe *that*, then you're dumber than I thought." I put a hand on my hip. *So much for the high road.* I begin to walk away, despite the fact that I wanted to wait for Peyton. But I just need away from the blonde spawns of Satan.

"Why else would he be staying here for the summer?" Blonde number one asks as she picks at her nail beds as if she's bored with this conversation. My heart slams into my chest and I find myself getting short of breath at her question. *He's…what?*

"He's staying here to be there for Alli and prepare for the baby," Blonde number two interjects. A smirk finds her face, and I'm sure they're both thrilled to have successfully ruined my night.

"I don't buy that for a second." *He's staying here? Like in*

DC? I know Alli is from Virginia, but what about his home? What about...me?

"Ask him then." Blonde number two sasses before they sashay away.

The two tequila shots I had suddenly feel more like ten, and they're swirling around my stomach and my brain and I feel like I need to expel them from my body. I watch as Everett makes his way towards me with a smile on his face, though I watch as it falls as he gets closer to me. "What's wrong, baby?"

My heart skips a beat. There's that word, *baby*. I can't tell if I'm happy to hear him call me that, or sad because it reminds me of the literal meaning of that word. A small child that he's having with another woman.

"I need to use the bathroom." I'm away from him and beelining for the ladies' room before he can respond. I push my way through the door, grateful that there's not a line and move into the stall, closing the door behind me. I put my hands on each wall to brace myself from the vomit desperate to leave my body.

He promised he wasn't going to play house with her.

He said he wanted me.

But you told him you didn't want him, my mind responds. My thoughts are interrupted by two high pitched giggles.

"Did you see the look on her face?" one voice says. "Too bad Alli wasn't here to see that, she would have been so satisfied." Hot tears bubble inside of me as I realize that it's the girls from earlier and they're talking about me. I sit on the toilet and raise my feet up to give them the sense that they're in the bathroom alone. Though I'm sure they're too drunk to notice or care if they did.

"Did you tell her that Everett's slutty ex is here?"

I put a hand over my mouth to muffle my cries. *Well, isn't* that the pot calling the kettle black. Actually, I'm not a pot or a kettle. I'm not a slut. I've slept with one guy!

MY FUCKING GUY.

I ignore the pesky voice in my head that told me that Alli was *technically* dating him while I was fucking him meaning I might be straddling that slutty line. *Pun intended.*

"No, it'll just make her upset, I'll tell her later."

"Are they really trying to work it out, though? I thought he was only staying here for an internship, and even then, he's still on the fence."

"Oh my God Hannah, can you get with the program? I wasn't going to tell *her* that. She needs to get the picture that they're *over*. Or else this would have all been for nothing."

My ears perk up and I lower my brows hoping that it'll help me decipher whatever code they're talking in. *What would have all been for nothing?*

"Yeah, well I didn't know Alli getting pregnant was part of the plan." One of them snorts. "I thought she didn't even fuck him." I put my hand over my mouth to drown out the scream bubbling in my throat when I hear the door open.

No no no no! I want to hear them! The loud shrieks of drunk girls enter the bathroom and I can't hear their voices over the noise. My feet find the ground and I try my best to peek through the door but I can't tell if they're still there. My phone lights up with a text message and I immediately know who it's from.

Everett: You okay in there?
Me: Yes…please don't leave. We need to talk.
Everett: Of course, I'm not leaving. I haven't talked to you in a month. I miss my girl.
Me: I've missed you too.

Everett: I started eating on the South quad that you eat at to avoid me. Took everything in me not to throw you over my shoulder and take you home when guys would eat with you and Peyton.

I don't respond to his jealousy because it's almost comical.
You got a girl pregnant. Me eating lunch with friends of Peyton's flavor of the week is hardly a reason to be jealous.

I peek my head out of the stall, to see a significant line has formed. I wash my hands and slide past the line and through the bar when I see my man leaning against the wall near the door. He looks so deliciously sexy it makes my knees weak.

Focus.

"Everett." I shake my head at him and then I push myself into his arms. I reach up behind his neck and bring his face closer to mine. I press a kiss to his lips, but I pull apart before he can deepen it. A smile is on his face when we pull apart and before he can comment on our first kiss in four weeks, I decide to drop the bomb. "Something's…wrong."

"What? What is it?" His face is laced with concern and when his hands gently stroke my face, the tears spring to my eyes.

"She…she did something. I don't know what." I let out a breath. "There—there's a plan."

"What do you mean?"

I take a deep breath as I calm my racing heart and prepare my thoughts. "I heard her friends in the bathroom. One of them said she wasn't even aware you and Alli had sex." I blink the tears away. "Don't stay here this summer, Everett. Come home to…Arizona. Come with me."

He rubs his jaw and his shoulders sink. "That's what this is about? And who even told you about that?"

"Alli's bitchy friends basically told me you guys are back together."

"We certainly are not," he growls.

Well, that's a relief, sort of.

I narrow my gaze in question. "But you're staying here with her this summer?"

"I'm not staying here *with* her. I was offered an internship and my parents thought it was a good idea. They want me to step up and be responsible."

"There may not be anything for you to be responsible for! That baby may not be yours, Everett."

He bites his lip and he looks out into the crowd. "I'm going to take a paternity test when the baby's born and—"

"No, you can do it now since it's been eight weeks. You need the truth. The way they sounded…it just didn't sound right."

"What girls, Leigh? Who said something to you?"

I look around the room, trying to identify them, but the room is getting more crowded by the second and I don't see them. "I…" I shake my head. "I don't know, but Everett I swear, I'm not lying."

"I don't think you'd ever lie to me," he says sincerely. His blue eyes are raking over me and I know he's reading me just like he's always been able to do. "I just think maybe you misunderstood, or maybe they were fucking lying to you to get under your skin and drive an even bigger wedge between you and me." He shakes his head. "Her friends are bitches."

"Birds of a feather." I raise an eyebrow at him and he has the decency to agree with me. "But no, I was in the bathroom stall and they were talking to each other. They didn't even know I was there. One of them said that Alli getting pregnant was not part of the plan, and the other said she had no idea you guys even had sex. Everett, something is off about all of this, and I think…I think maybe she's trying to trap you or maybe she's not even pregnant. Maybe this is all a fucking game. Have you even seen a sonogram or gone to an appointment with her or…"

He doesn't say anything; he just looks out into the crowd and my heart sinks.

"You have…"

"I went to her last doctor's appointment with her."

A tear slides down my cheek and he reaches up to touch it. I let him because I'm weak. I'm weak and I relish in his touch.

"Just when I think it can't hurt anymore…" I whisper. I pull out my phone to send a text to Peyton that I'm sorry but I'm leaving before I start moving towards the door.

"Leighton…I'm so sorry." He falls into step with me as we make our way outside. "But we are not together. I haven't touched her or kissed her or slept at her house or gone out with her or anything. I've been thinking about you since I left your house."

I start walking away from the bar when I hear my name being called. I turn around to see Peyton jogging towards us despite being in four-inch heels.

"You're leaving…?" She looks at me and then at Everett. No one says anything, though I know the answer to her questions are written all over my face, and in the body language between me and Everett. His hand is resting on the small of my back and I can sense I'm leaning into him. "You'll make sure she gets home safe?"

His eyes widen and he nods, and I'll admit that I'm shocked that she's so accepting of me leaving with him. She pulls me into a hug and murmurs into my ear. "I know you miss him. And I just talked to Dave and Pat who said he's been a miserable dick. This situation sucks all around, but maybe… maybe I was wrong about him. Maybe it really was just a mistake." She pulls back and shakes her head. "I'm not convinced one way or the other but…" She looks at Everett and then at me. "You two loving each other as hard as you do should count for something." She purses her lips and looks out into the warm summer night. "Hell, it may just count for everything."

Thirteen

Everett

THE WALK TO LEIGHTON'S HOUSE IS QUIET. THE SOUNDS OF Friday night swirls around us as we walk past the strip of bars and through the neighborhood of those hosting house parties. I'm wary of sliding my hand through hers because I don't want to push her. This is the first time we've spoken in a month and I'm worried the second I touch her, she'll shut down—or I'll attack her.

"I think you should take the paternity test sooner rather than later. There are much less invasive procedures to do that, now." She looks over at me nervously. "I googled."

I let out a breath, my mind still spinning by what Leighton said at the bar.

Is it possible that all of this has been bullshit?

I know she's really pregnant, but what if I'm not the father?

If this has all been some bullshit ploy, you can bet I'll kill Alli the second she gives birth.

And that's counting on the fact that Leighton doesn't beat me to it.

"What reason would she have to fuck with me like this? Fuck with us?"

She shrugs. "I don't know. To get back at us? Or maybe

she really does think it's yours. But I do think it's worth looking into maybe sooner rather than later. I just…I don't want to see *you* get any more hurt over this situation."

"It's only hurt watching this take its toll on you and *us*."

I've been forced to be without not only my girlfriend but also my best friend for the past month, potentially because Alli is a woman scorned?

"You've missed me too?" Her words cut through my thoughts and I recall what I said earlier. I turn my gaze to her to see her staring at the ground as we walk.

"Of course, I have. I don't think a minute has gone by that I haven't thought about you at least once."

She continues walking and I see her shiver making me wish I had a jacket to give her, though I'm sure it isn't due to the weather. Before I do something drunk and slightly chivalrous like taking the shirt off my own back, I ask her, "You cold?" She shakes her head, her gaze still fixed at the ground when I stop her. I grab her arms and hold her in place. "Leighton, look at me."

Her eyes meet mine and they're sad and defeated and it kills me that I may have broken her spirit. *Broken her.* I lean down, pulling her into my arms and stroke her back gently. "I don't expect you to forgive me, or accept all of this, but I just…I hope you'll let me try and make this right. I've been miserable without you the last month. I love you. I miss you."

She doesn't say anything for the remainder of our walk, and as soon as we're through her door and it closes behind us, she's on me. Her tiny body climbs up mine and wraps around me. Her legs twine around my waist and her arms around my neck and her lips are on mine before I can blink. Her force sends me back slightly as I wasn't expecting her to all but attack me and suddenly, I'm pinned up against the door. I cup her ass and she groans into my mouth as I walk her to the couch.

As soon as I sit down, a whine leaves her throat and when she pulls back, she yanks her shirt out of her skirt and tosses it across the room. "Upstairs!"

What she wants becomes painfully clear. And I say painful because the restraint I'm exercising is making my dick physically ache in my jeans. My cock is so hard, I think it could cut through the fabric *and the zipper* of my jeans because all it wants is to be back inside Leighton. *Where it belongs.*

"Wait, baby. Wait wait wait," I tell her, despite her sinfully tight body writhing against me. "Just one second." I pull her hands to my mouth and rain kisses over her fingertips.

"I don't want to wait. And I don't want sweet lovemaking. I want you to fuck me, Everett. I want you to put your mouth on my pussy and then fuck me like you've missed me." She rests her forehead against mine and lets out a deep breath. "I want you to fuck me," she bites her lip, *"there."*

My brain, which is telling me that we need to talk before we get intimate, is slowly getting on the same page as my dick, which is currently screaming at the idea of being inside Leighton's tight ass. I'd explored that area thoroughly with my mouth and my fingers, but she'd always been too nervous to take the step. Her springing this on me now, just reassures me that Leighton is feeling insecure and I don't want to take advantage of that vulnerability.

"Leighton..." I cup her face in my hands and despite the several drinks I had before she showed up, I feel myself sobering at the sad look on her face. The look that mirrors the pain that's been tearing her apart for months.

"You don't...want that anymore?" Her eyes widen and she sinks those teeth into those delectable lips.

"I do. Oh God, baby, I do." I grab her ass for emphasis. "I just, I think we need to talk before we go there again."

"I don't want to talk." She shakes her head and puts her hands flat on my chest. "I want to fuck, and I want you to have complete ownership of my body. I need it. I need you to possess me...fully. I need you to...keep me."

"I do possess you, Leighton." My voice is low and gravelly, as Leighton's words arouse the caveman in me that wants to guard Leighton with every ounce of his life. "You walked away from this. You broke up with *me*." I raise her chin to look at me. "And I understand why you did. But it doesn't mean that I stopped possessing you while we were apart. You'll always be mine, Leighton Mills, and there's not a damn thing anyone can say to make me believe differently. *Even you.*"

She whimpers and I watch as goosebumps appear everywhere, as my gaze continues to penetrate her. "I needed time," she whispers. "Time to figure out if this is something I can handle. Something I'm mature enough to handle." She looks away, breaking our eye contact, and she takes a deep breath. "The consensus is I'm not." She giggles nervously. "But...I am mature enough to understand that I love you *more* than I hate this shitty situation. I love you enough to be with you despite this relationship you have with another woman. You may be my best friend in the world, but you're also *my* man, and I'll be damned if I let you go without a fight."

Her words turn my already hard cock even harder and instinctively I flex up into her wishing we were both naked so I could impale her. *Hold on, Everett. Use your words before you pin her to the couch and fuck the life out of her.* "There's no fight. I'm yours." I grab a handful of her hair and yank it, exposing her neck to me.

"I meant," she gasps when I sink my teeth into her, "a

fight against myself. It'll be hard every day, and I can't promise I'll always be totally agreeable, but I'm going to try. I'm just asking that you be patient with me."

I run my tongue over where I just bit her and pull back slowly to look at her. "I'm the patient one," I tease and I note a red tinge in her cheeks. I think we both know that I have the patience of a saint, especially when it comes to her sassy ass, and it's her that usually is ready to blow the second I *really* tick her off.

She nods in agreement. "I want…I want to get back together."

And then the last of my resolve breaks. My lips are on hers in a second as my hands are unsnapping her bra. Her luscious tits spring free and I push her down onto the couch making her lie on her back. "Wait." She puts a hand up and I look at her in almost horror, that she's telling me to stop while her rosy nipples are currently pebbling under my gaze and aching for my tongue. "I want to go upstairs. Once we start, I don't plan on stopping and I don't know when Peyton is coming home."

I nod in agreement, just as I hear her phone chime from somewhere in the room. "It's probably just Peyton," she says dismissively as she searches the room for her discarded purse and pulls it out while I grab her shirt and bra from the floor. Her eyebrows form a V between her eyes and for a second, I think it's Alli, who I'm sure has gotten wind that I went home with Leighton, and if she's really as vindictive as her friends implied, she probably is trying to stir up more trouble.

I look over her shoulder and immediately see red with who texted her at damn near midnight. "Are you fucking kidding?" Her eyes snap to mine and look down at her phone. "Your ex-boyfriend?" *Why the hell is Adam texting her?*

She looks contrite for a literal second before she rolls her eyes. "He's going to help me study for the stats final." She grabs her shirt from me and pulls it over her naked breasts.

"Still doesn't really address my question of *are you fucking kidding?*"

"Everett…"

"That douche is texting you at midnight about statistics? Give me a fucking break, Leighton Alexandra." Even though it was brief, I definitely caught the *what's up?* Which at midnight on a Friday night is the fuckboy code for "you up? And can I swing through to *hang out* and potentially fuck your drunk brains out?"

She looks up at me with a devilish grin. "I love when you use my first and middle name. It makes me think I'm in trouble. And I *love* when I'm in trouble." She bites her lip and trails her fingertips down her neck, stroking the skin I love to wrap my hands around. The space I love to bite.

Fuck, I loved when she pisses me off enough for me to use her full name too. I shake my head, remembering why I'm pissed in the first place. *But hold the fuck up.*

"Are you hooking up with him? I mean…while we were apart?"

Her mouth drops open before forming an angry expression. "Why are you asking me questions you already know the answer to?"

She wouldn't. "Have you seen him…? Outside of class?"

"No, Everett, but he offered to help me study and I agreed. I need help."

"I'll help you. I took it last semester; I may still even have my practice final."

"You have your own exams to study for, and you're just doing this because you're jealous for literally no reason."

"He's your ex-boyfriend, Leighton," I spit out, wanting to break his neck for even thinking that he could get back with her that way.

"Nothing was going to happen, even if you and I didn't get back together, and now that we are—"

"I don't want you seeing him," I interrupt.

She raises her eyebrows at me and puts her hands on her hips. "Really?" She holds her phone out for me to take. "We aren't even remotely flirting, Everett. Here, look." I want to tell myself that I trust her. That I don't have the right to look through her phone, especially given my precarious situation involving another girl, but I have to see it. I have to know what he's been saying. I don't think she was flirting, but I need to see what *his* angle is.

I scroll through slowly, and breathe a quiet sigh of relief when I note it really all does seem innocent, mostly about statistics, and him asking her how she is. The questions are mostly one sided, and I'm happy that Leighton rarely kept the conversation going. I hand her phone back to her, satisfied but still far from thrilled at the idea of her spending an entire night with him preparing for her final.

"Yes, really, Leighton. You are *mine* and if I have to fuck the life out of you to drive my point home, I will."

"Don't threaten me with a good time, Cartwright." She smirks. And in this moment, I hate that I'm going to give in to what she wants, but I also know that I won't be able to fuck her without exerting my possession over her especially in light of this new information.

"I don't want you alone with him. Plain and simple." I take a step towards her just as she takes one back, and I can already see the playful glint in her eye.

She bites down on her lip and then turns and bolts up the

stairs. I'm behind her instantly, chasing her towards her room. I slam the door behind me as she hops on the bed, her sexy tits bouncing and making my mouth water. She pulls her shirt off over her head and pulls her skirt and panties down leaving her naked in seconds besides the smile on her face and the love in her eyes.

I lean up against her door, my arms crossed over my chest as I eye her lasciviously. "Come here," I command. She stands to her feet preparing to walk over when I put a hand up. "On your knees. *Crawl.*"

She blinks her eyes several times before she bows her head and slowly lowers herself to her hands and knees. She moves towards me putting one hand in front of the other and her knees move in tandem as she moves closer to me. When she's in front of me, she sits back on her heels and looks up at me, those dark eyes, almost the color of the night sky. I unbutton my jeans, letting them fall to the floor and rub my dick through my briefs before letting my hands fall to my sides. "Take it out."

She does as I ask without hesitation, sliding my black briefs down my legs and letting them join my jeans, which are still around my ankles. She licks her lips and I grasp her jaw, squeezing slightly.

"Stick out your tongue." She follows my command, opening her mouth so I can rub my cock across the pink, silky muscle. I let go of her jaw and she starts to close her mouth around me when I shoot her a warning glare. "Eager little thing, aren't you? You want me to shoot my cum down your throat?"

She can't speak because my cock is resting on her tongue but her eyes widen excitedly and she nods vigorously. Her tongue curls slightly rubbing the tip across one of the veins on the underside of my dick and I groan at the gentle stroke. "Goddamn, your mouth is so fucking sinful."

She closes her lips around me and I thrust into her eager, wanting mouth, pushing back slightly further each time. When I feel myself hit the back of her throat, I watch as her eyes water slightly and drool pools at the corners of her mouth. I feel puffs of air as she breathes through her nose and when I pull back out of her mouth she gasps for a bit of air. "You're doing so well." She smiles at my approval. "Tell me, are you wet? Is your pussy tingling and needy after having my cock in your mouth?"

She nods. "Yes."

"Let me see," I demand and when she sits back on her ass and spreads her legs I almost fall to my knees when that pink, slick flesh comes into view. I swallow when she spreads the lips obscenely, revealing her pulsing clit and the rest of her pussy. "Fuck," I whisper and suddenly I've forgotten about the blowjob and am desperate to get my cock inside of her wet cunt. "On the bed." I pull my jeans and underwear from around my ankles, yank my shirt off and I'm on top of her all within seconds. My body feels like it's on fire with need for her, and she seems to be feeling the same as she claws and scratches my back.

"God, I've missed you so much," she mewls when my cock bumps her sex. "My vibrator really can't do what you can." She half chuckles half moans when I tweak her nipples between my fingers.

"Ah yes, my arch nemesis." I press my lips to her shoulder, remembering that purple toy that sat in her bedside table that she used when I wasn't around. I feel her heart pounding against my chest as my body covers hers and I wonder if she's just extremely turned on or nervous as well. I press a kiss to her neck before continuing my trail down her body to her pussy. I run two fingers through her slick folds before bringing them to my lips and sucking her sweetness off of them. "I am going to eat this pussy until you don't know your own fucking name." I growl as I slide my tongue across her mound. I thought about teasing her, taunting her with the promise of an orgasm before I eventually let her succumb to the pleasure. But when I look up at her, her eyes wild, her hair teased, and voluminous from me pulling on it, I realize I want to make her come *now*.

And I know just how to do that.

I dive in, wasting no time before attacking her clit and sliding two fingers inside of her and curling upwards. "Oh God!" she cries out when I slide a finger in her ass as well. "Oh fuck. Oh fuck!" My tongue swirls around her clit, as I grind my dick into the mattress, humping it in time with each pulse of her clit. She's beginning to quiver around me and when I look up, she's staring at me through hooded slits. She grabs the back of my head and pushes her sex harder into my mouth and I welcome the explosion flowing from her cunt. "Yes! Everett!" she screams.

"So fucking wet," I mumble, as I submerge my face in her sex as she continues to ride the wave. "Say it," I grit out. "Say what I want to hear, Leigh."

"I love you." Her other hand moves to my head, cupping it with both hands before she tugs slightly and I move up her body. She puts my head in her hands and our eyes lock just as I slide into her. "I love you so much."

Our eyes locked in this intimate moment as I move in and out of her, almost pushes me over the edge. I've jacked off while we were apart, particularly on the days I'd seen her on campus, but being inside of her—having my dick in her mouth. Tasting her cunt, and the promise of what's to come between those delectable cheeks of hers has me barreling towards my orgasm way sooner than I want.

I pull out and sit on my heels. "Get on your hands and knees."

"Now...?" Her eyes are full of question and I shake my head in response to her unspoken one. "Not yet, I just want to fuck you from behind. Hands and knees. Don't make me ask you again." She turns to face the head of the bed before hiking her ass high up in the air and pressing her cheek against the mattress.

I run my fingertip between her cheeks and circle the ring back there before I push in gently. My cock which feels heavy between my legs begins to leak precum and my balls tingle, making me wonder if I could come just by touching her.

"Have you been taking your pill?" I ask her, hating that I'm taking us out of the moment, but knowing that I may not have enough restraint to pull out and the last thing I needed is another pregnant girl. Even if *she* would be the one I wanted to eventually knock up.

"Yes! Please fuck me. Come inside me!"

I groan at her request, her plea, her demand, and push inside of her hot cunt. "Oh my fucking God, how did I forget what this felt like?"

I've been inside Leighton thousands of times, and I still couldn't reach this level of pleasure when I tried to reenact it with my fucking hand.

Nothing felt like Leighton's pussy.

Nothing felt like Leighton.

"Your pussy is so goddamn perfect, it's like reaching *nirvana*." I rut into her almost erratically, chasing my orgasm with fast strokes. "Rub your clit for me, baby. Get it nice and hot. I need you wet and loose and languid so you're calm when I take this." I press my hand to her ass and she pushes back against it.

She may have been nervous before, but she certainly isn't now. I'm fucking her harder and faster now, my hands gripping her hips as I move her up and down my dick. The orgasm hits me hard and fast as it zips up my spine and grabs me by the throat leaving me gasping for air. "Leigh...fuck fuck fuck!"

I can hear her yelling, telling me how good I feel, how much she loves when I come inside of her, but it's muffled, and when I drop my head to her back, letting myself slip out of her I wonder if she came too with how hard she's breathing. I reach around and rub her pussy and she whimpers when I touch her quivering clit.

"Did we...we came together?"

She nods, like she can't speak either, and when she turns her head, I can see the tears in her eyes before one streams down her face. "Holy shit."

She's lying on her stomach, her teeth biting down on her pillow as I rim her, trying to get her as relaxed as possible. I've fucked her twice, while I probed her ass with two fingers and made her come with my mouth again as I entered a third finger, and now I believe her limbs are probably as loose as Jell-O. I pull away, the space between her cheeks wet and slippery from my spit as I press two fingers saturated with the warm gel against her hole. She shivers, the goosebumps rising on her skin and I press a kiss to her shoulder.

"You are doing so well, baby."

She lets the pillow drop from between her teeth. "No, *baby*. Not now."

"What should I call you then? You want to be my dirty

little slut?" I ask her as I continue to finger her asshole slowly stretching her.

"Yes." She shudders again and from this angle, I can see the ghost of a smile on her lips. "Yes, please. Talk dirty to me."

I push myself slightly into her and I feel her tense. "Relax," I whisper somewhat soothingly, letting her know that the man that worshipped her is still present despite what I might say to her. But I offset it with my fingers digging into her hips as I steady myself. I was ready to blow the second she'd agreed to let me fuck her ass, and now I'm one centimeter inside of the tightest vessel of my life and I'm ready to blow.

Everett, if you come already, I will never get hard again, I swear I can hear my dick telling me.

"Aren't you going to push?" I hear her whisper from below me and my hand smacks her ass in response.

"You. aren't. in. charge." I growl at her. "You don't get to ask questions."

"I'm sorry."

"Sorry for what?" I taunt her as I push further inside.

"Trying to be in charge. I just…need you to push, please!"

"And why is that? Because you're desperate for me to fill all of your holes today? You've already had my dick in your mouth and in your pussy and between your luscious tits. What part of your body hasn't my dick touched, Leighton? Is there any part of you off limits to me?"

She shifts underneath me and the sexiest simple sigh leaves her lips. "Nothing."

"Fuck," I grit out through teeth clenched so tightly I'm sure the veins in my temple are visible. I know she'd say something along those lines, but hearing the breathy word escape her lips has me barreling back towards the edge.

Calm. the. Fuck. down. You aren't even halfway in.

I push further, and she gasps underneath me, the moan sounding like music to my ears. "Everett, holy fuck." She clenches around me making my cock throb in her ass.

"How does it feel, Leigh?"

"I'm so…full."

"Does my little slut like having her ass fucked?"

"Y—yes. Yes, I like having you in my ass." She trembles underneath me and I groan because I can feel it in my dick. "It feels…like you own me."

"FUCK." My dick pulses again hearing those words, and I push the rest of the way in and a scream of pleasure leaves her body. I drop my face to her neck and press a gentle kiss to the space there just so she can feel that I'm still with her. "I'm going to start moving. Now." I growl as I begin to rock in and out of her. "Next time," I hesitate, as I get my thoughts together, "I'll have you sit in my lap so I can wrap my hand around your pretty throat while I fuck you like this."

"Oh my God, yes!" she screams. I feel my cock ready to blow for what I'm assuming will be the final time of the night, so I begin to rub her clit between her legs.

"Just give me one more, baby."

"Oh God yes, I want to come. Make me come, *please*." Her plea is enough to make me lose it. The strain in her voice, the begging for me to make her feel good makes me feel like a God, knowing that I'm the only one who can.

"I love you so fucking much, I'm never letting you go again," I tell her.

"Yes!" she screams as I swipe across her clit one more time sending her over the edge. "*Never* let me go."

Fourteen

Everett

"Excuse me?" Alli looks angry and disgruntled and livid, as soon as the words leave my lips. I've spent the majority of the weekend in bed with Leighton reuniting after so much time apart and the second Monday morning hit, I was armed with a new purpose.

To prevent anything from coming between her and me again.

Which means it is time to officially know the truth, and after her friends potentially outed what sounded like a fucking scheme, I want answers and I'm prepared to be ruthless in my quest for the truth.

So, I'd gone to the sorority house, and when they told me she was on her way home from her final, I decided to wait. She'd greeted me with a smile before I pinned her with a cold glare and told her that this was far from a social call.

She rubs her hands on her leggings and I watch the goosebumps popping up on her arms as a shudder rips through her. *Nervously.* "I take offense to that, you know. I haven't been with anyone else besides you."

"So, you say, but I'd like there to be no doubts and quite frankly, everyone in my life wants proof as well."

She snorts and rolls her eyes. "You mean Leighton?"

I scratch my jaw and narrow my gaze at her. "Yeah, I do mean Leighton."

"You said she was done with you…that you were done with *her*." Her voice wavers slightly.

"I've never said I was done with Leigh. *Ever*. And furthermore, that doesn't have shit to do with you. We are taking a paternity test. I'm actually not sure why we're having this argument. This was always the plan. I was always planning to request one when the baby was born. I'm just requesting to have it done now. I'll cover the costs since I want to do it earlier. You're further along than eight weeks; they can do a test with just a swab of my cheek and a blood sample. I just need the truth." I inform her. "And I have to say your extreme reluctance to do this is making you look guilty as hell. If you're so sure it's mine, then what's the problem?"

"The problem is you're making me feel like shit because Leighton is so desperate for this baby *not* to be yours!"

"ENOUGH about Leighton!" I yell, before taking a deep breath, counting to ten. I pinch the bridge of my nose and prepare to let her have it. "Jesus Christ, YOUR friends were talking shit to her at the bar on Friday, did you know that? YOUR friends slipped up when they thought she wasn't around and said something about you getting pregnant wasn't part of 'some plan?' What the hell is that, Alli? Is this all some game? My dad's a lawyer, and I can promise you it's not a game you want to play with his son," I growl at her and she shakes her head.

Tears spring to her eyes and she bites down on her bottom lip before she takes a step back. "I—I don't know what they're talking about."

"I think you're lying straight to my face, Alli. We're taking a test, *tomorrow*," I tell her, knowing that she has a doctor's appointment anyway.

155

She shakes her head, the tears threatening to fall from her eyes as she takes a deep breath. "Do you really hate me that much?" She wrings her hands nervously and I'm beginning to wonder if I've just been blind to the bullshit this whole time.

"Hate has nothing to do with any of this." I take a step forward, my voice low, cold, *hurt*. "Alli, is there even any point in taking this test?"

She doesn't respond, so I take another step. "Allison," I grit out her full name and she swallows.

"I...*yes?*" she squeaks.

"That sounds an awful fucking lot like a question for someone who was sure she'd only ever been with me."

"I..."

I take a step back, my mind going a mile a minute at her fear, her nervousness, her *uncertainty*. "Alli, did you sleep with someone else?" Her eyes flash to mine and I put a hand up. "I don't give a fuck if you cheated on me or not. I want to know if you slept with another guy. A guy who might be the father!" I point at her stomach. "You've turned my goddamn life upside down for the past two months KNOWING there was a chance this baby may not be mine? I know I hurt you, and I'm sorry. I get that you were upset. But you were going to what...trap me? Or what, Alli, did you think I'd just fall in love with you when the baby was born and not give a fuck that the test results showed that it wasn't mine?"

"I DIDN'T SAY IT WASN'T YOURS!" She screams.

"You certainly aren't convinced it is, anymore," I growl. Something Leighton says flashes through my mind. "One of your friends said she didn't know we fucked. That night...I was so drunk." I close my eyes, trying for the millionth time to trigger something from that night but it still comes up blank. "God, if I didn't know any better, I'd say I was drugged." I rub my head and as if the answer just fell out of the sky and landed at my feet, my head jerks up to meet her terrified gaze. "You wouldn't have," I say, but even as I say it, I realize that I'm not sure what exactly she *wouldn't* do to get what she wants. "Speak! Say something. Deny *anything*."

"I...I think you just blacked out that night. As did I! I don't remember anything."

"Bullshit! Oh my God, Alli, did you slip something in my drink?"

"No! How could you think that?"

"Well, to be honest, I don't know all that much about you, but what I've seen the past few months, I haven't liked very much. And surely not what I've learned the past thirty minutes. You've let me believe this is mine without a doubt, you've said multiple times that this couldn't be anyone else's, all the while knowing you fucked some other guy? That makes you a *bad* person, Alli," I tell her. "And I don't even want to know what it makes you if you drugged me the night we allegedly had sex. I'm guessing a felon. I'll have to ask my dad," I snarl before I turn and walk towards my car when I hear her scurrying behind me.

"Wait, Everett!" She puts her hands over her eyes and shakes her head. "Okay, we'll...we'll take the test."

"Oh, there wasn't a question in that. And I wasn't asking for your permission. I mean I guess I can't force you, but I can have a court summon it. I do know that I'm well within my rights to do *that*." I shake my head at her. "I didn't deserve this. For you to have done this to me?"

"And I deserved you cheating on me!?"

"NO! And I've said that many times. But this is a *baby* that you what...tricked me into believing was mine? I met your parents, you humiliated my girlfriend and pushed her away from me. I wasn't going to abandon you if this baby was mine, Alli, and if you would have just thought about this baby instead of your fucking self, you would have realized that Leighton would have loved this baby too. She's not a bad person, Alli. She's been in love with me for a really fucking long time. And I know you don't care, but for you to do this... it's unforgivable. If this test proves this baby isn't mine...then I'm going to go as far as to say that we probably didn't have sex that night. That you drugged me..." I put a hand up when she interjects. "Or maybe I did just get that drunk on my own, though I'm not convinced given that pieces of that night feel like they've been wiped from my memory...*but* I'm going to say that you went with it when we woke up naked that next morning. At the very least, *you're* not even completely convinced that we had sex."

"Everett..." She hiccups and wraps her arms around herself as a breeze whips through the air.

"I'll see you at two," I tell her before storming off towards my car.

I slam the door to Leighton's house behind me so hard it shakes. Peyton and Skyler, who are sitting on the couch with their books strewn across them, jump nearly three feet. "Oh my God!" Peyton shrieks. "Why?!"

I ball my hands into fists and close my eyes. "Leighton." The word leaves my lips like a prayer, and instantly I feel the tension leaving my body as if just her name has the power to calm me.

"She's at campus! She's studying at the library," Peyton says.

"Without one of you guys?" It isn't necessarily late, but I know studying for finals can take you way into the night, and I hate that she would have to get home by herself late at night.

"I think she's in a study group," Skyler adds.

"Don't you have like a chip in her to track her movements or something?" Peyton quips and gives me a smirk.

I put a hand up. "I am *really* not in the mood."

Peyton pulls a pencil from behind her ear and points at me. "Then you can exit the way you entered because you're in *my* house, Cartwright."

"Don't start, you two. What's wrong, Everett?" Skyler asks. "You're shaking."

"I...I need Leigh."

"Okay, well just text her."

"Do you know who she's studying with?" I'm not sure where we'd landed on her little study date with Adam, but I hope to God that she isn't studying with him.

For her sake.

My sake.

My fucking sanity.

Me: Hey, I'm at your house. Where are you? I need to talk to you.

Leighton: Library! What's wrong?

Me: Who are you with?

Leighton: Study group for stats

Me: With Adam?

Leighton: Everett...

Me: Are you serious?

Leighton: He's here, yes. But there's a lot of us. Like ten.

Me: I don't care. I told you how I felt about you being with him.

Leighton: I didn't think you'd be upset if I wasn't alone with him.

Me: Spending time with your ex-boyfriend in ANY fucking capacity, Leighton. You knew what the fuck I meant.

Leighton: Stop swearing at me! I'm sorry, okay? But I really don't want to fail this exam. It's worth like thirty percent of my grade. And he can't exactly take it like he's been doing my homework.

Me: Whatever. This day has been the fucking worst and now you're dicking around with your ex.

Leighton: Wow. I can't even believe you're going there. You're overreacting. I don't want Adam. I NEVER wanted Adam and you know that! And what's going on?

I stop answering because I know if we continue down this road while I'm angry over Alli and jealous over Adam that I'll end up saying something I regret and hurting Leighton. "Dammit!" I growl as I drop to their couch next to Skyler. She closes her textbook and sets it on the table in front of her.

She crosses her legs in a pretzel and looks over at me. "Care to share with the class?"

"Not really," I grumble.

"Too bad. Do you want a drink?" Peyton asks as she stands up and makes her way from the couch and into the kitchen. "Some of your beers are here." I shake my head as I let it fall into my hands.

"Everything is so fucked," I grumble.

"I'm guessing this is about Alli?" Skyler asks.

"And maybe also because my girlfriend is hanging out with that douchebag Adam." I look at Peyton. "Wait…aren't you in Leigh's statistics class? Why aren't you at the study group?"

"Organized study groups aren't really my thing," Peyton quips and Skyler snorts.

"Yes, cheating is more your thing."

"Says the girl who slept with her professor for an A?" Peyton retorts with a flick of her blonde hair over her shoulder.

She smacks Peyton's arm. "I did not *sleep* with Aidan for an A, bitch."

"Oh, I'm sorry, did you *not* get an A?"

"Because I'm smart as shit."

"And just maybe…*maybe* I'm good at math." Skyler turns her head and narrows her eyes at Peyton. "I'm good at stats okay? I'm thinking of minoring in it."

"You…like…math?"

"Don't make a big deal about it. The math section was what saved my SATs. I got a perfect score on that section."

Skyler's mouth drops open, and quite frankly I'm just as shocked. "Weren't you stoned?" I ask, having heard this story before.

"Obviously, but math doesn't change. I can do math while I'm drunk too. Don't tell anyone." She rolls her eyes and turns back to her textbook.

"Then why aren't you tutoring Leigh?" I snap at the revelation.

"Because she's stubborn and doesn't listen! Trust me, I tried. And then what's his face started doing her homework for her, so she didn't need my help anymore."

"We're getting off topic. Though I do want to know more about my best friend being a math whiz and me never knowing." Skyler points at Peyton before turning to me. "What's going on with Alli?"

"I don't think the baby is mine." I blurt out. "I wanted to

talk to Leigh first, but she's not here, and I have to get this off my chest."

Peyton crosses her arms over her chest and eyes me warily. "Go on."

"I think she drugged me the night we supposedly had sex. It's why I don't have any memory of it. When we woke up naked, she went with it. But I don't think we actually had sex. If we did, I definitely was not a willing participant. But…that baby…she fucked someone else in the interim. Or maybe she cheated on me. I don't know but…" I know I've been rambling and when I look over to Skyler and Peyton both of their mouths are open, their eyes wide. "Oh…oh my God," Skyler whispers.

"Oh yeah, we all need drinks." Peyton gets up and comes back with a bottle of vodka and three shots. "Holy shit, did she admit that? Oh my God, Leighton is going to kill her." She puts a hand on her forehead dramatically. "Oh my God, we're going to be accomplices to murder." She squeezes her eyes together before taking her shot. "Oh, you know what, I'm not worried. Between your dad and Daddy West we'll get off," she says looking at Skyler.

Skyler scrunches her cheeks upward and I've heard a vague story about Skyler's older sister, Serena's engagement to her dad's best friend and partner which is where I assume the *Daddy* term comes from. "I'm serious," I tell them.

"Peyton's serious," Skyler says as she downs the shot. "She knew this whole time the baby may not be yours? I spent a month picking my best friend off her bathroom floor because Alli wanted to fuck with you?" Her eyes fill with rage, and I'm beginning to think she's just as angry as me. "When are you taking the test?"

"'Tomorrow," I say before downing the shot Peyton poured for me.

"I almost pray it's yours," Skyler says.

"I don't!" I growl, not wanting to put that into the universe.

"Okay, I mean…I don't. I've been hoping this whole time it wasn't yours but…this is just so disgusting. She knew this whole time that there was someone else. And then if she really did drug you…" She crosses her arms. "I hope you're planning to press charges, and if you're *not*, then I wouldn't tell Leighton about any of this."

"She'll probably never admit if she did. It's not like I can prove it now."

Peyton lets out a breath just as I hear keys in the door and then Leighton is coming through it. She narrows her gaze at us and the shot glasses littering the table. "Is this studying?"

Peyton and Skyler hop up from the couch in sync. "You've got the floor, Cartwright. We'll leave you with the vodka," Peyton says before they bound up the stairs, leaving us alone.

"You…you didn't answer." She sets her bag on the couch and sits next to me, linking her arm with mine and leaning her head on my shoulder. "My last text. I didn't want you here stewing and being mad at me." She kisses my shoulder and looks up at me with those big beautiful eyes that have the power to completely alter my mood. I press a kiss to her forehead, and already I feel better.

"I'm not mad at you."

"You were…but I swear I wasn't alone with him. But he was there…" She bites her bottom lip.

"I'm not thrilled about it, but I'll live. Thanks for coming back."

"Well, I'm sure Skyler and Peyton would have wrangled me in when you guys got…drunk?" She raises an eyebrow and points at the three shot glasses between us.

"I learned some interesting news today, and they were kind of talking me through it until you got here." I let out a sigh, and she turns to look at me.

"Do I need a shot?" She rubs her thighs nervously and I grab her hands and pull them to my lips.

"I'll let you hear the news first."

"Okay…"

I launch into everything that happened earlier with Alli and when I finish, Leighton looks like she's going to be sick, but she jumps to her feet. "I KNEW IT! That conniving bitch!" She stamps her foot and puts her hands over her eyes, digging the heels of her palms into them. "How could she do this? Why? She needs help. Like professional help. She's certifiable."

"Okay, well before we go admitting her to a psych ward, I need to find out if it's true."

"The fact that she's been lying about only being with you, something tells me it's probably pretty true."

"Baby, come sit down. You're making me anxious." I need my hands on her, and given that we've always fed off of each other's emotions, her getting worked up is successfully getting *me* worked up. I need her calm, so *I'll* stay calm.

She comes back around and sits in my lap. "I know we've been hoping for this, but the way it sounds like this might play out, I'm in shock." She swallows. "I'd accepted the fact that the baby was yours."

I let out a breath. "Yeah, me too."

"Do you know who the other guy is?"

"No…I didn't ask. I didn't want to know, nor do I care. I'm not mad that there was another guy, obviously."

She nods and stares off into the distance. "Do you want me to come?"

"Yes…but also no." I begin stroking her hair, running the strands through my fingertips and letting her silky mane calm me. I stroke the skin on the back of her neck under her hair and she practically purrs in my arms. "I want you with me always, but…I don't want to worry about you flying off the handle. I think it's just something I need to deal with alone first." She doesn't put up a fight and just rests her head on my shoulder. "I just…I need to know…"

"Know what?"

"No matter the outcome…" I start.

She flips her wrist over and shows me her tattoo. "No matter where, no matter what."

Fifteen

Everett

We're sitting in the waiting room of her doctor's office; a chair between us because I moved the second she tried to sit down next to me.

"You're being really childish, Everett," she snaps and her icy blue eyes flit around the waiting room to the other expectant mothers, and she can't be serious if she thinks that I'm going to put on some fucking show or even *appear* cordial to her right now.

"I wouldn't start, unless you really want to see how childish I can be." I watch as a mother in the corner gives me some significant side eye, and I fight the urge to tell her to mind her business.

She sighs defeatedly and presses her fingertips to her temples. "Everett…can…can we just not do this here?"

"Are you going to tell me the truth? About anything?"

"I've told you as much of the truth as I remember."

"Have you?" I ask her. "Because anytime we talk about anything, I feel like you've been vague and you try to talk me in circles."

"I haven't, I—"

"Allison Jeffries?" Her name is called and I'm on my feet instantly, following her back to the examining room.

Here we go.

Two days. That's how soon I'll have an answer about whether I'll be a father or not. I cross my arms over my chest as we walk to our respective cars. "Who's the other guy?"

"Does it matter?"

"No, but I mean...does he know he might be a dad?"

She swallows, and I look at her wondering what's causing her silence. "I tried reaching out and..."

"And he ghosted you?"

She lets out a sigh. "I didn't tell him anything via text, I just said we should talk. He didn't respond."

"Was it only once?"

She leans against her car, a white BMW, and picks at her nail beds. "More than once."

"While we were together?"

"Everett, we weren't sleeping together...you wouldn't touch me! And you were so obsessed with Leighton! Do you know how much it hurt that it felt like my boyfriend didn't like me? I was lonely and jealous and...he paid attention to me."

I rub my head. "I don't care that you were cheating on me. I care that you've been such a goddamn hypocrite about me and Leighton."

"I didn't care about this other guy. It was just sex! I cared about you!" she exclaims, shooting her hands in the air exasperation.

"Oh. That makes it better then. I'm the asshole because I've wanted to marry Leighton since I was nine years old though." My lips form a straight line and I bob my head up and down. "I'm glad we've got that cleared up." I snort.

"Look," she lets out a sigh, "I was drunk." A tear rolls down her cheek and she brushes it away with the back of her hand. Her cheeks turn pink, and her teeth chatter slightly. "And upset, and I did care about you. I had just gotten dumped and everyone knew you were just there that night as a pity date. I tried to ignore how obvious it was that you loved Leighton, and the fact that you'd dumped me for her. I thought I could make you forget about her." She wipes her face. "My friends made a joke about drugging you and making it look like we messed around. They were going to take pictures and we were going to send them to Leighton." I see red. *I would have ruined every last one of them.* "You don't understand, I was hurt and so hammered." She puts a hand over her eyes, and I know if I snap now, I'll never get the full story. So, despite the fact that I want to rip her head from her body at this confession, I stay quiet.

"But I told them no. I told them I didn't want to do it. I wanted to just let you go and forget about you. Maybe spread a rumor that you had a small dick, I don't know." She lets her head fall back and stares up into the sky. "I didn't drug you, Everett."

"But one of your fucking friends did?!" My outburst causes her to find my eyes again. Her eyes are sad and tired and remorseful.

Unlucky for her, I'm in no mood to grant forgiveness.

"I don't know, and none of them have owned up to it. But…you say you don't remember and…I was so drunk. I don't think we had sex. I just assumed when we woke up, and…"

"You fucking bitch," I growl. "I can't believe you kept this from me for months! For what?!"

"BECAUSE I WAS SCARED! This baby *is* real, Everett. A very real baby, I didn't fake that. This wasn't immaculate conception. This is *someone's* baby! And for a while, I thought it was yours."

"Except you didn't think you fucked me," I growl.

"I'd been sleeping with the other guy for about a month and then that night happened and...I don't know! I was confused! Then I thought maybe we did?"

"Forget my relationship with Leighton that this almost ruined. You almost ruined my life! Even if you thought we did have sex, I deserved to know about everything else. You tried to play me for a fucking fool!"

"I know! I know. And I'm so sorry, Everett." She cries.

"Is there any chance this baby is mine?"

"Yeah, there's a chance...we may have tried that night? I don't...I don't know. It's all so blurry!"

"But knowing all of these facts three months ago would have been really fucking helpful." I shake my head, thinking about everything I've been through the last semester. "Why are you just telling me this now? I mean what were you going to do in nine months if we waited till the baby was born? You couldn't have thought that I would have suggested we just be some big damn happy family."

"I guess I was thinking...hoping, you'd get attached to me or the baby and you'd want to stick around and help or just be there."

"So you were trying to manipulate me. Not trap me because that would require a court to make me do something which would require proof of paternity."

"No! I just..." I shrug. "I don't know. I'm telling you now because I watched you in there. I've been watching you for the past month. You're so unhappy." Her face falls. "I did that to you and I'm sorry. But I don't want to bring a baby into a world where I'm causing this kind of pain. I don't want my baby to have a mother like that."

"Well, it will."

She winces at the harshness of my statement. "I'm telling you now."

"Because you're caught! Because in two days the paper is going to say Everett Cartwright 99.9% not a match for Alli Jeffries' baby! Why are you making it seem like this is some moment of clarity and you're doing the right thing?!"

"I am *trying* to do the right thing!" She argues and I can hear the desperation in her voice to try and get me to see that.

"When we get these test results, pending that I am not the father, I will probably never speak to you again. I'm not going to press charges for whatever bullshit you and your friends potentially did to me. I just want you out of my life."

"Fair," she says sadly.

"I don't wish bad things on you Alli, and I hate that the other potential father doesn't want to be involved. I don't wish that for you. But this is the worst thing anyone's ever done to me and I won't be forgiving you all that easy."

"I know." I look away from her, this enlightening conversation weighing down on my shoulders. "I am sorry, Everett." When I turn to her, her eyes look sincere, but I don't know if it's all an act. The phrase way too little and far too late flashes through my mind, but despite my anger, I just want it to be over. I don't want to argue with her anymore.

"I know you are, and I'm sorry that I hurt you, in any capacity."

It doesn't excuse what she did, but I am sorry. I don't want her baby to be born into a world where it has to witness men hurting its mother. I want better for this new life that maybe I didn't help create but have thought about quite a bit the past two months.

I want better for all of us.

Leighton is sitting on my bed next to me as I hold the envelope in my hands. When I got home two days ago and broke down and told Leighton everything, I practically had to pin her down and sate her with orgasms to calm her. She was ready to burn the sorority house to the ground, and I can't say I wouldn't have handed her the matches.

She rubs her nose on my shoulder, and I turn to look at her. She holds her wrist up as she snakes her hand up my shirt and rubs the tattoo on my side. I nod in response to her message. After we'd made love for hours, we'd had a long talk about a lot of things. In light of this new information, it did seem like the chances that I was the father were slim, but we wanted to wait until we had everything in black and white. I'd informed my parents, leaving out the part about being drugged because I knew that was the fastest way to get both of my parents out here. Though I wanted to keep it from Leigh, I couldn't, and I know it's taking every ounce of restraint she has not to tear Alli a new one and go to someone high up in the Panhellenic Council to report what happened. Maybe nothing would come about without proof, but the seed would be planted and at very least an investigation would be conducted for any kind of paraphernalia in the house.

Leighton's wearing one of my lacrosse sweatshirts and she rubs the sleeve against her lip. "Don't be nervous," I tell her.

"I'm not. No matter what, I'm not going anywhere," she tells me and it makes me think we really were meant to be together forever. If we could get through the past two months, we would get through anything. My eyes flit to her left hand, picturing the ring I've already picked out sitting proudly on her finger.

Her eyes follow my gaze to her hand and then looks at me. "One day," she whispers. I grab her left hand and rub her ring finger before pressing a kiss to the knuckle, and she smiles before grabbing my face. "I love you," she whispers.

I press my lips to hers before turning to the envelope again. I tear it open, revealing the one sheet of paper folded into thirds neatly. I open it up, steeling myself for the results and I hear her gasp the second I read over the words.

Not. A. Match.

I read over the words over and over and over, making sure I'm not hallucinating or my mind isn't making me believe what I want to see and not what's actually there.

"Oh my God!" Leighton is off the bed and jumping up and down. I look up just in time to see her flying at me, wrapping her body around mine and kissing me passionately. "That means I'll get to be the mother of *all* your babies."

"Fuck. I'm not…just you…just you." I chant as her hands reach for my shirt pulling it off of me and forcing my shorts down. I yank my sweatshirt off of her revealing a tank top underneath and no bra. I immediately latch down on her breast and suck the nipple between my teeth, wetting the white fabric with my tongue. I rip her tank down the center, pushing her breasts together and running my tongue over the dark pebbled nipples. I pull her shorts and panties off and then she's on top of me, riding me. *Hard.*

I reach up, holding my hand around her throat and I pull her down so that I can whisper in her ear. "Mine. Fuck, you're so mine."

"No. You're fucking *mine*." She growls between thrusts and me letting her throat go ever so slightly. I roll us so that I'm on top of her and squeeze slightly. She grips my hand, squeezing it around her throat, and I know she must be getting light headed because she's squeezing down on my cock so hard. I can feel her juices dripping out of her and down my balls and I already can't wait to suck her hot clit into my mouth. I continue to thrust, feeling myself nearing the edge. "I…I…love… you…" she blurts out before her teeth sink into her bottom lip and she squeezes her eyes shut. I can feel her pulse in her neck flickering against my palm, and it's moving in sync with the pulsing in her sex.

"You come for me, Leighton Alexandra. You come for me right the fuck now."

"Mmmm," she whimpers.

"You come for me, so I can give sweet little kisses to your pussy. Would you like that?" I growl in her ear as she nods her head vigorously. "You're doing so good, coming for me like a good little slut." I let her neck go so I can bite her at her pulse point and the second I do, she explodes around me.

"Oh God, YES! Yes yes yes!" she screams. She pulls at my hair and pulls me away from her neck and latches her mouth to mine. "Fuck me fuck me fuck me." She arches her back off the bed and I think her orgasm is still going based on how hard she's squeezing me so I reach between us and rub her clit and she practically breaks the skin when she runs her nails down my back.

"Fuuuuuckkkkkk!" I groan at the delicious pain causing me to unleash my seed inside of her. I pump and thrust rope after rope of hot cum inside of her. I don't know how long I'm coming, but at some point, I feel myself soften inside of her and pull out begrudgingly from my favorite fucking place.

"God, you are sex personified, Leighton Mills. You're going to be the death of me."

Her body that was previously taut and stretched and tight, is now loose and languid and lying beneath me under a layer of sweat looking like a sex goddess.

"Fuck, that was so good." She giggles as I pull her into my arms. She rests her head on my chest and I begin to stroke her hair as she runs her fingertips over my torso.

"Marry me," I whisper into the room.

She freezes and looks up at me, confused. Though, if I know her like I think I do, she'll say *yes* despite my completely impulsive, completely unromantic, ringless proposal. "You're asking me now?"

"Will you? When I ask?"

"What do you think?"

"I think I want to hear you say it."

"I love that you ask, like I have some sort of choice."

I chuckle at her humor and pinch her side. "Leighton."

She doesn't say anything for a moment before she looks up at me, love and lust and adoration shooting from her eyes as she nods her head. "I'd marry you tomorrow, Everett Cartwright."

Leighton

Six Months Later

My heels click against the marble tile of the hospital as I move through the halls with the small pink bear in my hand preparing myself for when I hit room 404. I make it to the door and stand there for a moment before I knock twice.

"Come in!" I let out a breath and push through the door. I see who I assume to be Alli's parents, and a guy in the corner holding a pink bundle and then I see Alli in the center of the room on the bed, looking like she'd just gone for a light jog. *Of course she'd look gorgeous right after labor. Bitch.*

No. Be nice.

"Hi! Are you a friend of Alli's? I'm Alli's mom." She smiles and I smile back despite how uncomfortable I am.

"Leighton?" I hear Alli's voice.

"Hey…" I look around the room, and I pray that no one knows who I am. "I ummm…I heard you had the baby, and I just…I thought I would stop by."

It was impulsive. I was on my way to meet Skyler, Aidan, and Everett for drinks now that the three of us are twenty-one and seniors. The four of us have become pretty inseparable and go on double dates at least once a week. I'd say Peyton is about ready to kill us, but something tells me those double dates were about to turn into triple dates soon.

"I'll have to say I'm surprised to see you," she says softly.

"Well…ummm…" I hand her the pink bear with the phrase *You Are Loved* written across its stomach. "I wanted to bring the baby something."

"Do you mind giving us a second?" Alli says to the three other people in the room. The guy hands her the pink bundle before they disperse leaving us alone. "Do you want to see her?" she asks, and I nod once before making my way closer to the bed.

"She's so tiny," I whisper. "What's her name?"

"Isabella." She looks down at her and I can see the love shining from her eyes to this precious baby she'd brought into the world. "Listen, Leigh, thank you for coming. It was… really big of you."

"Yeah, well...I wasn't exactly innocent in all of this either."

"I know you hate me, and with reason, but I am sorry... for everything. Maybe you'll never forgive me, but I hope that one day you can." I didn't come for apologies or to hash anything out with her. I came for me. I came so that I could look at the one person that had tried to hurt me and break me, and pray that I didn't feel anger.

But I don't. I feel relief. I feel peace.

"It all worked out in the end." I give her a smile. "I am glad that you're happy."

"I am, Leighton. And I hope you're happy too."

"I am."

"Tell Everett I said hi?"

I nod before giving her a small wave, and then I'm out of the room, letting the door close behind me and on a chapter of my life that I thought I'd never be able to close. I make my way through the parking lot when I notice a familiar face standing against my car with a smirk across his face.

"How'd you find me?"

"I could find you anywhere." He smirks.

I wrap my arms around the back of his neck and press my lips to his. "Find my Friends?"

"My best friend." He corrects and my heart flutters just like it always does when I remember that I am the luckiest girl alive to be in love with her best friend. "You see Alli?"

"And Isabella. She's really cute for a newborn."

"You saw the baby?"

"The one that was almost yours?"

"It was never almost mine. Wrong eggs." He points at me.

"That was romantic and weird." I shake my head and bump his shoulder with mine. "I took her a bear."

"That was nice. You aren't fleeing a crime scene though, right?"

"Shut up. We apologized to each other." I smack his chest and he chuckles. "Did you want to go in?"

"No, I'm just here for you." He smiles before cupping my face and swiping his lips across mine. "I'm proud of you."

"For not killing her?"

"Well yes, but also for how much you've grown. You're an incredible human, Leighton Mills, and I'm lucky as hell to call you my best friend."

"You're getting sentimental on me. You're not proposing, are you?"

"And she has to ruin it." He rolls his eyes. "Meet you at the restaurant?"

I blow him a kiss as he walks away. "Hey," I call over our cars and he turns to look at me, "you're pretty incredible too, and maybe if you're lucky I'll do some pretty *incredible* things to your dick tonight." I wink before I hop in my car.

Epilogue

Leighton

Three Years Later

I can barely see through the tears as I watch the second line appear on the pregnancy test indicating I'm *pregnant*. I put a hand to my mouth as a smile crosses my face. I stand in the bathroom in our apartment in Georgetown that we'd gotten once we graduated with some help from our parents. Everett and I got married earlier this year and we are currently looking for a bigger place now that we are trying for a baby.

And now I'm pregnant!

I squeal as I peek my head out of the door. Everett and I have plans to go out to dinner tonight, but I have a feeling once I reveal this news, we will be spending the night celebrating at home *alone*. I look down at the test and wonder if I should plan a fun, cute reveal. I think about that for about a half a second before I realize that it would require keeping a secret from Everett for longer than four seconds, which is impossible. I'd accidentally spoiled two surprise parties for him, *one of which I'm planning* because I don't know how to keep a secret from my man.

"Everett, Everett!!" I squeal as I make my way out of

the bathroom and into the living room where my husband is nursing a beer and watching a Thursday night football game. "Everett."

"Mrs. Cartwright," he addresses me, reluctantly pulling his eyes from the television and roaming his eyes over me. He gives me a smile, one of those sexy smiles that are reserved only for me before turning back to the game.

I dart my gaze to the fifty-inch flat screen mounted on the wall that Everett about threw a fit in the store to get, knowing damn well it basically dwarfed our small living room inside our small, but very expensive apartment.

"I need to tell you something? Can you..." I point at the television but he still hasn't looked back at me. "Babe!"

"It's overtime, baby, five minutes."

"Five minutes in football? What, is there only twelve seconds left on the clock!?" I stamp my foot and turn to the television and then back to him.

"Come sit here. Come sit in my lap." He taps his lap and I narrow my gaze. Irritation floats through me, but the idea of sitting on Everett's lap sends a sexy shiver through me.

Maybe I can play with his...

I'm already moving before I can finish the thought and I'm in his lap, pressing my lips to his neck and rubbing my hand down his chest and over his dick that is hidden by a pair of sweatpants.

"Oh, hello." He chuckles and rubs my back, but I can see he's still looking at the game. "OH COME ON!" he yells.

"Everett." I wince at the volume.

He presses a kiss to my forehead before turning back to the game. "Sorry, baby."

I know the chances of me being able to get his attention now is slim, so I decide to just drop the bomb. "Speaking of baby, we're having one." *Well, that's not how I thought that was going to go.* I roll my eyes and giggle at my delivery.

Whatever, I'll do better on the next one.

He turns from the television and looks at me. "Say what, now?"

"Surprise!" I hold up the stick, I'd been hiding in the pocket of my joggers.

He turns the television off immediately and stares up at me and then down at the stick and then up at me again. "We're having a baby? You're…you're pregnant?"

I nod as tears spring to my eyes again, and then his lips are on mine, his tongue rubbing against mine gently and then roughly. "Leigh," he whispers against my lips, his hand finding my stomach and rubbing the space gently. He slides his hand up my body to cup my face before he pulls away from me. "You're so fucking amazing." He rubs his lips over my tattoo before he lifts me in his arms.

"We're bailing on dinner, right?" I ask him and he stares at me with wide eyes before shaking his head.

He shoots me a wicked grin. "You'll be lucky if I let you out of our bedroom before Sunday."

THE END

Author's Note

So originally, Spring Semester was supposed to be a completely different story. Some of you may remember I was writing about my real-life friend? But it turns out that writing a true story is actually really hard! Who knew!? I struggled with staying true to their story and stirring up the drama where it was needed. So, I decided after what felt like a month of writer's block to tell a different story.

One about two best friends that had in been in love all their lives and now that the truth is out, they don't know how to deal with each other. And because you know I love all things forbidden, Leighton and Everett demanded to be dating other people at the time. Spring Semester was my angstiest ride to date and I hope you enjoyed their story as much as I loved writing it (and really diving into some of the college experiences I didn't in First or Second Semester!)

Thank you so much for reading!
Xoxo,
QB

Acknowledgements

This book wouldn't… *couldn't* have happened without some pretty fabulous people. Your input, your love, your support is invaluable to me. As I, (and Carrie Bradshaw) have said probably a million times—sometimes family is the one you're born into, and sometimes it's the one you make for yourself.

Carmel Rhodes, Thank you for helping me through what felt like the most painful writer's block ever. For talking everything out with me, and helping me make sense of all of Leighton and Everett's crazy! I have no idea what I'd do without you and your constant pushing and mom-aging. Love you big time.

Helen Hadjia, Leslie Middleton, Melissa Spence, Kristene Bernabe, Erica Marselas, Harlow Layne, Kristina Loaiza my insanely thorough betas, you've been with me for quite a while at this point and I don't think you even understand what it means to me. I love you guys so much for everything you've done and do for me every day. You continue to show up for me and for that I'm so grateful!

Jeanette Piastri, where do I begin? Thank you for helping me bring all of my book babies to life over and over again. The cover is gorgeous and thank you so much for all the pretty things you made for me!

Kristen Portillo & Stacey Blake, thank you for making my books sparkle and shine every time. Your magic never ceases to amaze me!

Kelsey Cheyenne, Danielle James, Gemini Jensen, Rose Croft and Alexis Rae, thank you for all of your feedback and advice and sprinting with me when I need it! I'm so lucky to be on this journey with such badass women. I love you RR!

Denise Reyes, I am so freaking grateful for you. For talking with me about everything book related and for being in a different time zone which means I can message you at two in the morning and you'll see it! For being such a genuine sweetheart and cheering so many of us on! You rock and I love you!

To my author friends, I'm so lucky to know you and I can't thank you enough for your friendship and advice and support! I love you so much and I can't wait to meet and squeeze all of you (some later this year!)

To everyone in the Hive, my sassy babes! Some of you have been with me, what, almost five years? Where does the time go? Thank you for your love and your support and making me feel like I *can*. I love you!

And finally, to the readers: Thank you for going on yet another journey with me. You guys rock my world every day!

About the Author

Write. Wine. Work. Repeat. A look inside the mind of a not so ex-party girl's escape from her crazy life. Hailing from the Nation's Capital, Q.B. Tyler, spends her days constructing her "happily ever afters" with a twist, featuring sassy heroines and the heroes that worship them. But most importantly the love story that develops despite *inconvenient* circumstances.

Sign up for her newsletter to stay in touch! (http://eepurl.com/doT8EL)
Qbtyler03@gmail.com

Facebook: m.facebook.com/author.qbtyler

Reader Group www.facebook.com/groups/784082448468154

Goodreads www.goodreads.com/author/show/17506935.Q_B_Tyler

Instagram www.instagram.com/author.qbtyler

Bookbub www.bookbub.com/profile/q-b-tyler

Wordpress /qbtyler.wordpress.com

Also by
Q.B. TYLER

My Best Friend's Sister
Unconditional

BITTERSWEET DUET
Bittersweet Surrender
Bittersweet Addiction

CAMPUS TALES SERIES
First Semester
Second Semester

Printed in Great Britain
by Amazon